"In this engaging novel, Mitch Beam returns to a small town to mine its stories and ends up writing his own. Blending history and mystery, comedy and tragedy, *Scuffletown* depicts the triumphs and foibles of a cast of unforgettable eccentrics whose quirks reveal rather than undermine their humanity. It's a delightful contribution to Southern literature that understands how people talk, how gossip works, and how the social fabric is woven. It's also a thoroughly absorbing story that's hard to step away from."

Elise Blackwell, author of <u>Hunger</u>, <u>The Unnatural History of Cypress Parish</u>, <u>Grub</u>, <u>An Unfinished Score</u>, and <u>The Lower Quarter</u>, http://eliseblackwell.com/

Only in a small southern town, in the era of Lynyrd Skynyrd and Pontiac GTOs, will you find the characters and events Tommy Cofield creates so lovingly in his debut novel. Horse traders, teenage pranksters, a preacher-hypnotist, a spirits-selling soothsayer, even a two-headed dog romp through *Scuffletown*, where you can be haunted by a Little League mishap as much as the local Civil War-era ghost. If you grew up in such a place at such a time, you will be right at home. Get a six-pack of PBR and prepare to laugh – this is the funniest book I've ever read.

Aida Rogers
Editor of <u>State of the Heart</u>: <u>South Carolina Writers on the Places They Love</u>

There's nothing quite like a good story about a small town and its interesting people. The fictional town Tommy Cofield has created has similarities to so many of these wonderful places to live but also has its own unique, mysterious qualities. Tommy offers us a creative, intriguing novel that is an enjoyable read and keeps you involved from the first page to the last.

Dr. Ben Davis
Former Mayor of Fountain Inn, SC

SCUFFLETOWN

SCUFFLETOWN

a novel by

TOMMY COFIELD

Palmetto Publishing Group
Charleston, SC

Scuffletown
Copyright © 2020 by Tommy Cofield

First Edition

Printed in the United States

Dust Jacket: 978-1-64111-869-9
Paperback: 978-1-64111-803-3
eBook: 978-1-64111-870-5

Published by
Palmetto Publishing
in conjunction with Misfit Press

Cover Photography by Erin B. Wackerhagen
Cover Interior Design by Palmetto Publishing

For my family, Janet, T.J., and Caitlin,
who encouraged and inspired me, often.

Tell the truth, even though that's not exactly the way it happened.
—Flannery O'Connor

A light come from my head
Showed how to give birth to the dead
That they might nourish me.
—James Dickey, *The Island*

NOTE TO THE READER

This book is totally a work of fiction; therefore, it is the fruit of the author's imagination. Although real places, historic figures, and sometimes real events appear in the story, all the characters and the storyline incidents are composite figments. Anyone who attempts to identify or interpret a character as a depiction of himself, herself, and/or anyone else who has ever walked among the quick will be guilty of vain phantasmagoria.

—The Author

PART I

CHAPTER 1

August 10, 1975

About halfway down the steps of the double-wide, Bud Culdock felt a knee lock coming on, so he grabbed the rail and shifted over to his better leg. From his rented space at the edge of the tree line, he could see rolling hills and rows of ripe muscadine vines all the way to the banks of the Enoree River. On this mid-August morning, he surveyed Constan Hendershot's vineyard as if the whole farm belonged to him. As he listened to a hidden dove, the harvest tractor interrupted with a groan and gasp.

He bent and pressed the puffy ridges on both sides of his kneecap until the pain subsided. The tattooed numbers showing just above his T-shirt collar were the birthdates of his two daughters. Social Services had yanked them away long ago. He wore just enough face scruff to cover old acne scars, and his countenance was a skillet layered with old burn.

After a few minutes, he limped down the steps to his car. He rolled down the window and pulled out a ball cap tucked between the seat and the console. It had some remnant of blue to it and a pale circle marking where the Chicago Cubs logo used to be.

He had rescued that 1965 Thunderbird convertible from Shumate's Junk and Treasure following a multifatality wreck on Scuffletown Road. He bought the salvage and modified it with some newfangled air-conditioning. He advertised that it had "the coolest air in Dixie." He named his one-car taxi fleet the Chicago Cabs in honor of his beloved baseball team.

His plan was to take the morning off on cabbing. Just make a simple drive to his shoe shop in town. He had a few deadlines. A torn pocketbook strap, a pair of work boots, and the usual heels and half soles. Before he got in the taxi, he peeled away the magnetic logos and tossed them into the back seat. He lowered the canvas roof and put on his cap.

A cumulus trail mushroomed as he backed up and turned around. He coasted past the Hendershot mansion helipad and tennis courts, topped the hill near the old Jones corn mill, and then picked up a head of steam in order to cross the Enoree River Bridge. The river separated Spartanburg County from Greenville County, its first-cousin rival. The Enoree always seemed muddiest there at the bridge. That morning the air was cool but extra hazy, which he found a little odd.

Before turning onto Scuffletown Road, he filled up with gas at Henderson's Stop-N-Go and remembered to redeem a coupon for a large coffee. He set the cup into the holder, which he had rigged from a PVC pipe ring and soldered pipe hangers and duct-taped to the dashboard so that it doubled up as a taxi meter rack.

Before he could drive away from the pump, the owner, Tim Henderson, lifted his hand as if hailing a ride. He sidled up to the driver's side, reached out, and attempted to place his Braves cap over the Cubs cap. He pulled it back and let out a laugh that sounded like a shovel going through clay. "B.C., when you gon change that taxi name…it's too Yankee-fied. Take my Braves cap…help ya revenue."

"Ain't got time to play today," Culdock growled and then stepped on the accelerator and left the station. He looked back just once.

Tim put his cap back on and pulled his shirt over his belly as if he were Glad-Wrapping a loaf of Sunbeam.

Once onto Scuffletown Road, a two-lane with no painted lines, he picked up speed and zipped through a flicker of shade and the morning's first shafts of light. He had an uneasy feeling that something extraordinary lay ahead of him that day.

With the Gilder Creek Bridge about a quarter mile ahead, he was looking almost directly into the sun, but when he dipped into an area of dull shade, he saw what looked like smoke or steam seeping from something. As he got closer, he saw that it was the front hood of a gold automobile.

He steered off the road, and the tires crankled over the high weeds. He stomped the emergency brake. He pushed the door and jumped out and without any wasted motion tossed the coffee. Cup and all. He trotted at first, and despite the knee pain, he began to run toward the disabled car. Its motor wheezed. His knees shook. When he looked inside, he wished he hadn't been the first to find them.

CHAPTER 2

August 1985

Things just happen on Scuffletown Road. That's what Mitch Beam knew as he prepared to end his seven years of self-imposed exile. His white '72 Cutlass Supreme barreled on, and he felt every road patch as the bald tires pummeled along.

Scuffletown Road was an old wagon trail that connected the Newberry trade post in the middle of the state to the Dark Corner region in upper Greenville County. Dark Corner had no formal boundaries, and it once featured dense forests laden with tunnels, caves, and even elaborate tree dwellings. It had always been a refuge for an array of malcontents, fugitives, lawbreakers, moonshiners, Civil War deserters, and even the bounty hunters who stalked them.

Scuffletown Road still followed alongside the steep banks of the Enoree River, which the Cherokees called the river of muscadines. It crisscrossed a host of springs, marshes, and tributaries that sustained it: Horse Pen Creek, South Tyger River, Flat Rock Springs, Gilder Creek, and Andy Jones Springs.

Canopies of ash, hickory, oak, and sycamore trees obscured broad stretches of the river, which was chock-full of tasty bream, crappie, catfish, and redeye bass.

For unknown reasons, the trail bypassed the prosperous river post of Harmony, once the region's busiest commercial center. It angled away instead to the northeast toward the abandoned Cherokee villages at Crow's Point and Holly Springs. Harmony, claimed by the locals to have built the first covered church and school in the upstate, was named for the circuit-riding Methodist preacher-missionaries who wanted to encourage goodwill and also to bear witness to the harmony of the Gospels.

In 1850, an interloping Charleston plantation owner, Benjamin Franklin Stairley, purchased and cleared expansive sloping parcels on both sides of the trail. His impressive plantation became the model for prosperity. It featured the first known successful implementation of terraced rows for growing and irrigating. The awestruck sharecroppers and neighbors revered the plantation mostly, however, for the mansion Stairley constructed at the highest point of the property. It took over six years to complete, and the three-story, cypress-sided marvel was esteemed as the House of the Seven Chimneys.

The name for the wagon trail itself was conceived from still another innovation that originated on Stairley's plantation. On autumn weekends following the summer harvest, the wives of the Scotch-Irish sharecroppers would pool their food resources and stage multifamily and sometimes multivillage feasts.

Customarily, when the eating subsided, and always after sundown, the cooler temperatures of the piedmont evenings settled in, and the men would eventually slunk away cradling their swollen bellies, homemade blackberry pies, and jugs of madeira and muscadine wine. They liked to congregate around a sprawling sandbar that formed along a bend of Gilder Creek. Somehow the drinking escalated into arm-wrestling challenges and fistfights. Over time the fighting evolved into a looser, no-holds-barred mix of boxing and wrestling. They called it "scuffling." It had its own gentleman's code of honor for fighting and scoring, but it was the duration of the cheers and the volume of inebriated onlookers, rather than formal judges, who determined the victors. It was based on the Scotch-Irish maxim: the vote of the crowd is the real vote.

Scuffling soon became entertainment for every weekend. Spectators and combatants swarmed around the riffle on Gilder Creek that eventually became known as Scuffletown. They came from almost every settlement, farm, and community, and it quickly overtook card playing, cock fighting, and liquor chugging as the gambling favorite.

In the weeks after the burning of Columbia in 1865 by General William T. Sherman, the stately House of the Seven Chimneys brimmed over with the finest furniture, artwork, and inventions of the era. All the windows made the mansion gleam from its perch above the nearby wagon trail.

In the course of a few hours on a blustery spring evening, however, a rogue scout regiment from Sherman's army found the plantation, torched it, and reduced it to ashes and crag-rubble. They also destroyed the surrounding barns and servants' quarters and carried off most of the stored feed, crops, and livestock.

During that same night, Stairley and many of the indentured farmers who fought to protect him and his plantation house were lynched or shot. Stairley's wife and daughter, away visiting family in Charleston, were spared. A few of the survivors recounted how the soldiers tied up Stairley and tortured him by dragging him behind two horses. One of the sharecroppers, who later that evening had his eyes gouged out, swore that the soldiers had Stairley drawn and quartered by four of Stairley's own plantation horses. The terrified animals flung his blood, organs, and tethered limbs into the darkness, including down the southbound route of Scuffletown Road. Another horse, Stairley's favorite, scuttled and kicked its way up the northbound route, and neither the horse nor Stairley's chained remains were ever seen again.

CHAPTER 3

Now, all these years later, Scuffletown Road had a few signs but still lacked painted lines. Only rutted-out shoulders that tapered at the paved edges. The ching-ching of gravel against the underneath chassis and the swooshing and knocking of dandelion bulbs and pine and scrub-oak saplings all served as a driver's only indicators for when a vehicle was on or off the pavement.

Mitch was running late for Billy Cole's funeral. Scuffletown Road was the quickest way to get from the interstate to Rocky Creek Baptist Church. That was how he caved in on going that way. He kept replaying what he remembered about the phone message, which gave him the news about Billy.

"Hey, Bud…it's ya old plumbing boss, A.P.…I gotcha number from somebody, I can't even remember his name…but that don't matter…I hate to be the one, but I bet you ain't heard yet…here goes…it ain't like we didn't see it comin'…still hit us like a ton a bricks…it's Billy…he passed sometime yesterday…he died at his Aunt Shelby's…I ain't got all the details yet…but anyway he's gone…finally…it's a blessin' in my mind…that kind a sufferin'…he ain't sufferin' now at least. Anyway, service is bein' held at Rocky Creek Baptist tomorrow at one…I hope you somewhere close by and can make it in time. I knew you'd wanna know…I'll look for ya up in the balcony…just in case."

His chest ached as soon as he heard it, and he felt like heaving. The hour-and-a-half drive from Columbia had provided plenty of time to think about Billy, including why their friendship had faded. For Mitch it had played out like an overnight thunderstorm that he completely slept through, almost as if it never happened. He smiled thinking all the way back to when their orbits first crossed. Back in Little League baseball.

—

It was the last game of the season, and undefeated Tex-ize had already clinched the regular-season championship. Last-place Her Majesty hadn't won a single game and had scored only a handful of runs. Myron Parsons, a twelve-year-old man-child, was their only impressive player, and it was his pitching that would occasionally keep the score respectable.

"Tex-ize STINKS...Tex-ize STINKS..." Myron's teammates chanted from the dugout. He stopped warming up in the bullpen and watched them shimmy their way up the backstop fence as Tex-ize took their pre-game infield warm-up. Her Majesty continued to chant until they found a place near the top to perch. Their brown jerseys oozed through the chain-link fence holes like peanut butter on saltine crackers.

The Tex-ize Chemical plant's main holding pond, a two-acre cesspool, was only about one hundred yards from the ballpark. Whenever there was any appreciable breeze, the aroma and sometimes even clumps of cesspool bubbles would lift heavenward, hover, and then plop onto the playing field.

The Her Majesty players eventually slid down the backstop and formed a new battle line along the dugout fence. They began a counterpoint of per-cussion by flapping the slack spots in the fence.

In cleats Myron was six foot two and north of two hundred pounds. Even at age twelve, he loomed over the other players and most coaches too. His cleats covered the Carolina clay pitching mound like scuba flippers. At Little League mound distance, he could intimidate by almost touching the batter when he released a pitch. His other weapon was that he was well known to have streaks of wildness. He routinely beaned a handful of op-posing batters in every game. And that usually set off bawling spells and hollering mamas.

Under a barrage of hoops and boos, Coach Satterwhite escorted four-foot-one Mitch Beam toward home plate. Coach bellowed loud enough for the whole ballpark, "You just crouch-n-crowd...crouch-n-crowd...get in his big ol' head out there...make him hit ya no-zone..."

Several of Myron's warm-up pitches sailed way over the catcher's out-stretched mitt and whapped against the backstop. The Her Majesty in-fielders stopped their own warm-up tosses and chattering.

Myron stepped to the top of the mound and toed the rubber. Mitch cat-walked into the batter's box. He crouched and crowded the plate just like Coach told him. His helmet was almost even with the catcher's mitt.

Suddenly, Myron went into a corkscrew windup and let loose a two-seam fastball that would have been knee high and barely inside to any oth-er batter. But with Mitch's head jutting past where most knees would have been, the pitch easily bolo-beaned him in the left ear-flap. The velocity cracked the helmet, and the baseball shot all the way into shallow left field.

Coach Satterwhite ran to his wounded lead-off batter. He kept re-peating Mitch's name and slap-patting both cheeks. When Mitch finally opened his eyes and sat upright, Coach waved over his on-deck batter, Billy Cole, and proceeded to jaw with the Her Majesty head coach and several of the Her Majesty parents.

Mitch's first clear thought was about the peculiar warm flow in the vicinity of his privates. He instantly knew the unthinkable had happened. His eyes shot downward, and he saw that the baggy flannels had somehow bunched up away from his leg and underpants. If he could somehow get to his feet and keep the flannel from touching against his legs, he could avert disaster.

Coach and Billy Cole pulled him up to his feet, and he made a sub-tle pinch-pull to maintain the space under the flannel pants. The Tex-ize crowd and players cheered and then immediately returned to squabbling with the Her Majesty coaches. Mitch stutter-stepped and did a stiff-legged walk into the dugout. He caught sight of the water bucket. He checked his pants several more times. He shuffled toward the water bucket.

Kippy Barnette, who had lost his second base starting spot to Mitch, sat in the shaded other side of the dugout and had perfect vantage to ob-serve the ebb and flow. When Mitch made it all the way to the bucket, he feigned a loss of balance and wiggled his grip on the dipper, sending water across the front of his pants. Instantly, the disenfranchised teammate un-coiled and delivered his venom: "That ain't water...that ain't no water... that's pee...yep that's pee-pee right there...peed in his pants...old pee-pee pants..."

In the commotion, Mitch quickly dipped and dropped another full ladle square in the crotch, and he spread the spilled water all around the crucial spot.

Billy Cole held up his hands, walked toward home plate, and turned to the entire cast of players, coaches, umpires, and spectators. He could have been an evangelist preacher wrapping up a sermon to extend an altar call. "No siree...I seen it...listen...I seen it all...that ain't nothin' but spilt water..."

Billy spun around and trotted back into the dugout. He swiped the dipper from Mitch, ladled up another full cup, and flung it all over the front of Kippy's pants. Then he dropped another one across the front of his own uniform and then ran once more toward home plate. He extended his arms again. "Let's play some baseball."

CHAPTER 4

Mitch was within a couple of miles of reaching Scuffletown Road, and his thoughts easily shifted to Fountainville's most famous high school sweethearts, Myron Parsons and Lori Leigh Cole, Billy Cole's beautiful older sister. In the summer of 1975, the two beloved teenagers were found dead in a 1965 gold Pontiac GTO. The engine was running as hot as August asphalt, idling and parked halfway into a hollowed-out gap between rows of plum and persimmon trees. "Carbon monoxide." That was how the coroner officially wrote it up. It was also how the *Greenville News* described it, but the hows and whys that led up to it, and the rumors that followed, all remained as ill-defined as the road Mitch was returning to.

Auburn-haired, chocolate-eyed Lori Leigh Cole was always Miss Everything. Prize-winning prodigy pianist, three-time Bible Drill state champion, class president every year at Fountainville High School, and also the career points and assists leader on the girls' basketball team. In her junior year, she auditioned for and won the lead role of Opal in the community theater production of *Everybody Loves Opal*. It was a musical about a ditzy but loveable optimist who remained cheerful and kind even to the characters who schemed to kidnap and harm her. Her performances brought spillover audiences and saved the Fountainville Town Theater from a financial shortfall. Her notoriety also helped her land several more roles at the larger community theater in Greenville. She became known as Opal, or as "the girl who played Opal," and she was the unofficial princess of the town.

As Mitch drove onto Scuffletown Road, he also thought some more about Myron Parsons and how they bonded after their Little League bean-ball incident. Athletic Myron excelled at all sports but mostly golf. He told Mitch and others that he had his eyes set on the pro tour, and he spent most of his waking hours on the golf course. He spent most of his other spare time tinkering with his gold Pontiac GTO. He was known for drinking a little too much beer, gambling for spending money, and playing Motown music way too loud while driving. He also worshipped Lori Leigh Cole.

When Lori Leigh first went out with Myron, weighted down by his reputation for bad behavior and particularly for antagonizing local law enforcement, the undercurrent of town opinion evolved from initial shock to eventual resigned acceptance. Everybody loved and trusted their Opal.

—

At a quarter after one, Mitch was still a good five miles from the church. As he closed in on "the spot," as the locals still referred to it, he had the intense pull to keep on driving. Something else, though, maybe his own crush for Lori Leigh or maybe the reverence for that area of the roadway, compelled him to let off the accelerator. He drifted to the shoulder. The plum tree grove that once obscured Myron's GTO was completely wiped out. The surrounding land, which he believed was still in the Gilreath family, was boundaried by a barbed-wire fence and a padlocked gate. Two identical signs flanked each side of the gate: NO TRESPASSING—AND THAT MEANS YOU!

No wailing emergency vehicles. No remnants of crime-scene tape. No camera flashes. No markers. Not even a single roadside cross. He couldn't grasp what he expected to find there, but he needed to find something. Something way more than the ruts of a red clay driveway leading up through a field of weeds toward the shrouded farm home of the Gilreath family.

As he sat there, he closed his eyes and pieced their faces and voices together. Lori Leigh, Myron, and Billy. He also knew there was no holding back the competing thoughts of his own uncertain future, including where his next paycheck might come from.

—

Two weeks earlier, Mitch was in Atlanta, and he was concentrating on balancing his cheeks on the front edge of a leather sofa. He was waiting for the receptionist to wave him into the adjoining office. He watched cigarette smoke sail from the threshold, and he nervously coughed three times and gulped to stop the fourth one. Black-and-white photos of Judge Smack Jack and other actors and sports celebrities covered most of the wall space. A boom-box-size gavel balloon hung under the ceiling fixture and appeared to rise and drop in rhythm with the bounce of the ceiling blades. He gave a half smile to the receptionist. She looked down at her fresh manicure and did not look up again.

THE JUDGE SMACK JACK SHOW sprawled in two swoops of metal letters across the door. They seemed to hang heavy, as if their adhesive would give way to the first good wind gust.

He rubbed his palms across his pants legs, and he was recalling the first time being summoned in for a pep talk. He had only been trolling cases for the show for about a month. Success was spotty. As for the two smaller cases that he had struggled to sign up, the judge passed along the word that their potential was "boring and vapid."

A buzzer burst from the reception desk, and she pointed to the door without speaking. Mitch slid off the leather sofa and moved toward the door. He knocked, just in case.

In just those few seconds, his mind wiped its slate, and he lost track of everything he planned to say.

He needed stress relief.

"Beamer! Ya damn numbers…they look like shit. Really, worsen that… raccoon shit." The judge's right-hand man and kneecap buster, Elkin Bayne, already had two cigarettes going when he burst in. One at his desk by the phone, and the other in his hand. Mitch tried not to stare at either one.

"Bad timing, boss…bad luck. I got some leads…don't worry."

"Well, Judge ain't too keen on cutting slack. Especially for trollers," Bayne barked.

"I'm hearin' ya…" Mitch said.

Bayne waved his hands out in front as if he were stopping a car going down the wrong side of the highway. "It's my ass if I can't redeem *your* sorry ass. Don't make me have to cut bait."

Elkin reached into his desk drawer and pulled out a pair of fingernail clippers. He cupped them in his right hand and fanned out his other hand like an executioner standing at a gibbet. He didn't look up.

Mitch couldn't tell if Elkin was finished with him, but he walked out fast just in case there was more.

—

Mitch pulled forward along the shoulder, waking up dust and embedded stones. He looked at his watch and knew that Billy's funeral service, even if it started a little late, was already in full swing. He pressed the gas and thought even more deeply about the story of Lori Leigh and Myron. The loose ends, gossip, and rumors. The painful uncertainty of whether the complete details would ever come to light. In that moment, he saw the whole story through troller eyes, and he began to consider the commercial possibilities.

CHAPTER 5

Just as soon as Mitch entered the church parking lot, the organ thunder rumbled up through the floorboard and into his legs. He made a parking space in the grass between the horseshoe pits and walked a little faster than usual toward the stained-oak doors that dominated the front of the church. A bronze marker had been sawed in two and nailed to both doors at eye level:

ROCKY CREEK BAPTIST CHURCH:
ALL BIBLE, ALL DAY
SINCE JUNE 16, 1950,
AND THEN TO JUDGMENT DAY

The door whomped shut behind him, and he creaked on tiptoes for about ten paces through the vestibule, then over to a side door that seemed to aim toward the balcony. An usher shot out from behind a spray of flowers.

"You ain't missed much. They were late with the body. Then somebody hurled. Right there on the front steps. It's the heat. Plays hell on everything, don't it? Scoot on up. They ain't but one or two up there. Oh…we run out a programs…they only printed a handful."

Only one other person occupied the balcony. It was A.P. Thackston. Mitch and Billy's old plumbing boss. Even in the middle of a prayer, Mitch saw that A.P.'s eyes were wide open. Mitch slid into the other end of the same pew, and he watched A.P. tilt his head and spit a tarry stream into a Coke can that had its top lopped off.

The crowd below stood and sang the first verse of "Amazing Grace," which Mitch was pleased he could still remember. Without any warning, the preacher signaled for a drop to the fifth verse, and that threw everybody off kilter. Patches of voices sang words that tumbled to the finish line at different times. The preacher wasted no time giving the Irish blessing for a benediction and almost leaped down from the pulpit. He shook hands with those who from a distance looked like Billy's family members. He saw Shelby Shillinglaw, Billy's aunt. The preacher motioned to the pallbearers with one hand and waved for the others to follow. And right in the middle of the sanctuary, the preacher removed his robe to reveal a lime golf shirt, white Bermudas, and loafers with ankle booties.

Mitch looked at A.P. and shook his head as if he were about to question an umpire's call. He stood and pulled the seat of his pants and whispered to A.P., "Piss-poor send-off, if you ask me."

A.P. walked toward him. "Don't worry. You didn't miss nothing."

Mitch crossed his arms. "Tee times and long eulogies just don't mix, do they?"

"Let's head on down," A.P. whispered.

Mitch led the way down from the balcony single file until the casket blocked them at the bottom step. They were trapped.

Finally, A.P. spoke. "You and Billy...y'all 'bout twenty-four, ain'tcha?" His voice chain sawed through the vestibule. Mitch watched several familiar faces swing around with snappy precision. He stood in place and didn't answer A.P. "You know it's been almost ten years...ten years to the damn day we lost Lori Leigh and Myron."

Mitch watched with uncertainty as one of the pallbearers jaunted back inside toward him and reached to shake hands. Mitch was caught off guard and couldn't name the face.

"Mitch Beam...Mitch damn Beam...and damn if we was just talkin' about you and Billy and that two-headed dog. Yeah, a two-headed dog. You and Billy...yeah, I'll never forget that." The pallbearer spun and skipped outside and lifted his side of the casket.

CHAPTER 6

Over the two years following Lori Leigh's 1975 death, her daddy drank and pilled himself to death. He left Billy a note apologizing for choosing the coward's way for suicide. A few months later, Mrs. Cole dropped dead of a heart attack with Lori Leigh's glossy theater photo clutched to her breast. When Mrs. Cole died, there were only two remaining family members: Lori Leigh's brother, Billy, and her mother's sister, Shelby Shillinglaw.

Myron's parents, Rosa Lee and Myron, Sr., moved inconspicuously out of Fountainville about six months after the tragedy. They told a few neighbors that they just couldn't bear to live around so many reminders. They relocated to Saluda, North Carolina where Mr. Parsons started a golf club repair shop, and Mrs. Parsons, a retired music teacher, continued to give private lessons in piano and voice.

———

Once they were outside, A.P. led Mitch over to the only spot of shade behind the church. They stood there for a few minutes, and Mitch studied the group as they milled around Billy's hearse. Mitch knew what was coming. Most likely it would be A.P., but he knew it would be somebody soon enough. Once anybody gets brash enough to move from a small town, going home is always a pinched-up face asking where you're living and what you're doing. But spoken more as a statement than a real question.

"Now, somebody said something' 'bout you being some kind a 'troller,' *con*-troller, some kind a deal like that." A.P. spit into his can again. "And something about a TV show...where you livin' nowadays?"

"If you don't mind letting me stay with you a few days, I'll tell you all you'd ever wanna know about it. You okay with that?"

"Damn straight. If you don't mind a messy house. Divorce is a shit-storm, Bud. You lucky. You just keep stayin' lucky. That's all I'm sayin'."

"Hey, that ain't Culdock's old taxicab, is it?" Mitch asked, feeling a small rush.

"Well, there it is. Bigger than the world. Jump in the truck, and I'll take you to graveside. We'll go right past Culdock."

Mitch followed A.P. toward the truck and smiled when he read the slogan decal: THACKSTON'S PLUMBING—WE'RE MORE THAN PIPE DREAMS. He climbed in, and A.P. cranked up and immediately wedged his way into the procession line.

"You see any kind a law up there?" A.P. extended himself through the window as far as he could go.

Mitch locked his eyes on the cab, but he didn't see Culdock. "Ain't it always the way...how Culdock just always seems to hang around? Spanish moss. Yeah, he's like Spanish moss."

"I guess. But where's the law? Damn poor send-off for Billy, just like you said. This town always does an escort. Always. It's got Chief Swanger written all over it."

On its own, the hearse began to tug its mourners toward Scuffletown and Barbrey Cemetery. It skimped along like an injured newt shedding and regenerating a torn tail all at the same time. Light flickered through a thicket of mimosa and oak branches, and Mitch had more time to dwell on past things. Mainly a water jug and a fumbled dipper.

Without any warning the truck hit a pothole, jolting him back to the Judge Smack Jack studios, the aroma of cigarette smoke, and the sheen of Elkin Bayne's fingernail clippers.

CHAPTER 7

All around Barbrey Cemetery, there was just enough of a brewing thunderstorm to lift the leaves and flap the loose edge of the graveside tent. Mitch heard "God" and "peace" a few times, but only when the preacher turned his head in the right wind direction. Most of the thirty or so mourners looked down and wore shades and never acknowledged Mitch in any way.

"A.P., I tell you what I've learned so far about comin' back home. When a donkey ups and travels across the ocean to see the queen a England, he will not—I repeat, he will not—return as a racehorse."

A.P. turned and waved to somebody on the other side of the casket vault, and Mitch wasn't at all sure that A.P. had heard him. He waited until the preacher finished the closing prayer, and he was just about to speak up again when he heard a familiar voice.

"Look out now. Sometimes…sometimes you go to graveside, and you might find all kinds a things. Maybe even the ghost a Mitch Beam and A.P. Thackston." Rusha Goldsmith had hawked down out of nowhere. He wasted no time flinging his arm around Mitch's shoulder, and he clamped down so tight that Mitch couldn't breathe or speak.

Rusha Goldsmith, whose name was not supposed to be spelled like the country, was a puzzle with lost pieces. Nobody in Fountainville knew his for-real age, or when and how he came to town. It was believed by some that he was the illegitimate son of someone in the royal family of the king of Liberia, but Rusha was suspected as the source of that rumor.

Rusha never smoked, and he was quick to point out that he had no wrinkles. He routinely ran wind sprints and ate a strict diet of pickled eggs and cinnamon toast for breakfast. He never ate lunch. Supper was a broiled catfish platter and one glass of brandy. He slept with the window open, even in winter. And each night he would drift off to sleep listening to his collection of Al Hirt and Charlie Spivak records.

Mitch was a little surprised to see that Rusha was still alive, since Rusha was proficient as a bookie, running with women, and flim-flamming. Until the onset of golf carts, he enjoyed a long employment stint as the caddie chief at the Whip-Poor-Will Country Club. He was also Myron Parsons's personal tournament caddie. He had the gift of encouragement, especially for hot-tempered Myron, and his skill for reading greens was legend.

Once Mitch broke loose and welled up enough breath, he wiped his forehead and turned to Rusha. "Rush...you feel that breeze? I love comin' up here. Feel that nice piedmont kind a breeze. And a touch of fried chicken ridin' up in it."

Rusha laughed. "Wipes out a multitude a hot, don't it?"

Mitch wanted to keep talking, but it didn't seem like the right time or place. He decided to pull Rusha toward him like he was huddling to call a complicated pass play. "I might wanna get with you in the next couple a days. Catch up on some old times...Myron, Billy, and all. You willin' to do that?"

Rusha straightened and stared toward something way beyond where Mitch was standing. To Mitch's eye, Rusha looked like he could once again be in the middle of a fairway with Myron Parsons asking about yardage and the both of them arguing about the right club. After a few seconds of silence, Rusha leaned into Mitch's left side and nudged him toward a shadier spot away from the funeral crowd. They stood there for a minute or so.

Rusha broke the silence. "When Myron Parsons comes to mind, I think about them gamblers. And Myron gettin' all caught up in it." Mitch saw Rusha look down like he'd spilled soup in his lap.

Mitch was surprised. "Gamblers? What kind?"

"Golf ones. Easy pickins for Myron Parsons." Rusha snickered a couple of times, but it stopped abruptly.

"And you caddied?" Mitch wanted to be certain Rusha was relying on firsthand information.

"Seen it all. My own eyes *and* ears," Rusha said, and Mitch saw that stare from Rusha again like he might be watching a movie. "You see, Myron had this knack a gettin' in they heads. Next thing you know"—Rusha popped his palms together—"they right in his hip pocket. Stick a fork in 'em."

"What was it?" Mitch wanted to know.

"Nothin' more'n whistlin' a tune sometimes." Rusha chuckled.

"Got to be something more'n that," Mitch said.

"It was. It was. Most times it was a Ray Charles tune. Yep. He'd get to whistlin' 'Born to Lose,' real low at first. Then he'd get louder, and them gamblers, all of 'em, tryin' not to let they faces show it, but they couldn't help but hear it. I can just about hear Myron whistlin' right now."

"That don't seem all that much." Mitch wanted to know if there was more to it, and he waited for Rusha to speak.

"He had this other thing. You might see Myron do this sometimes on the last hole. Up and out the blue, he would just cold shank a shot. Or three-putt. Take two or three to get out the trap. Somethin' crazy like that. So that would cost him some cash, losin' that last hole. And after watchin' Myron do that a few times, I was puttin' his bag in the trunk, and I asked him about it."

"You sayin' he had mercy on 'em?" Mitch asked, thinking he had found another reason to like Myron Parsons.

"Oh, hayell no," Rusha snapped. "He told me this, and I can still hear his words. 'You got to think long term, Rusha. They gotta leave the course believin' they got a chance next time. Leave some fish in the pond, Rush. Leave some fish in the pond.'"

"Myron made some good money then?" Mitch intrigued by Myron's success and wanted to know more.

"Me too, you could say," Rusha said. "The more he made, the more I made. Caddie commission. Ride that pony is what I say. Ride that pony. But then that one time. One a them gamblers acted out."

"Fistfight, I bet. Rolling on the grass fight?" Mitch asked.

"Damn pistols, what I'm sayin'. This little skinny dude wearin' these sissy plaid pants. He lost big. He was the one squared up on us when we was leaving in the GTO. 'Bout fifty yards past the front gate. Myron had his Al Green music goin' on, I hear this pop-pop ding. An' I told Myron I heard a bullet on metal. So he gunned it till we was way out a range. We stopped and got out. Looked her up an' down all around. No signs of a bullet hole. But I know what I heard. And I thought I even heard a third pop, and later on, we found out that third pop was John Willie, the green superintendent. I was told he took his own heater and with one shot winged that old gambler's shootin' hand. Shut him down for good."

"Y'all take it to the police?" Mitch asked.

"Po-lice? Swanger? Gamblers? Never even came up. We didn't wanna get John Willie in any trouble. Would a made things worse. And all of it, about two weeks before Myron and Lori Leigh passed. You know what Myron did with his winnings that day? After my hundred-dollar tip and then a fifty-dollar bill for him, he took a big wad a cash to the nursing home. He told 'em to buy flowers for all the folks and keep the rest for a rainy day. Lookin' back…you know, Myron finished on a high note. Maybe even as high as Charlie Spivak playing triple C. You do know who Charlie Spivak was, don'tcha?"

CHAPTER 8

When they got back to the church, A.P. handed Mitch an extra key to the farmhouse. "Now when you pull in, you'll see a Beware of Dog sign. Don't whack out. It's all for show. Just go on in, grab a beer. I picked up the wrong-size pipes, so I'm headin' back to Fillipelli's. Look for me 'bout six."

A.P.'s family farm was a former working blueberry farm located on Scuffletown but outside the town limits. Mitch drove out of the church lot onto Scuffletown and coasted past what everybody knew as Typhoid Crossroads.

In 1965, according to what Mitch's daddy had described many times, there was a community-wide typhoid fever epidemic that caused the whole community to be inoculated and quarantined. Ten people died. Even though Mitch was only four at the time, he remembered people lining up for typhoid shots, and mostly how his arm burned and swelled to twice its size.

About a half mile farther down Scuffletown, Mitch crunched onto a gravel driveway. It encircled the historical marker in front of the Scuffletown USA Dance Barn. He got out of the car to read the short narrative about Benjamin Franklin Stairley and his House of the Seven Chimneys.

As he struggled over what kind of angle of the Lori Leigh-Myron story he could possibly develop for the show, he decided to walk a little farther to see if the scuffling sandbar was still present below the Gilder Creek Bridge.

When his hike ended about five minutes later, he peered over the bridge rail down into the overgrowth of poke salad leaves and cattails.

Other vegetation closer to the water was so tangled that the rapids were muted and visible only through a few gaps in the Kudzu. He squinted and stared for a while trying to discern creek from weed, and he remembered a part of a rhyme that the town prophetess, Sharona Riddle, used to say as a fallback answer for just about any situation. *"Ev'rybody* soon 'nuff finds / the river of the muscadines."

CHAPTER 9

Later that evening, as the two of them closed in on finishing a six-pack, Mitch could see that A.P. was shifting in his Barcalounger and fumbling boiled peanut shells all willy-nilly to the floor.

In the summer of 1976, the year after the death of Lori Leigh and Myron, A.P. formed Thackston Plumbing, Incorporated, and he hired Mitch Beam and Billy Cole as his first summer helpers. Mitch smiled thinking back on his first day on the job. Caterpillar-lipped with his first mustache and wearing a yellow Elton John T-shirt. Later that same day, A.P. saved them from permanent construction-site infamy after they unwittingly left footprints on a freshly set sidewalk. A.P. took all the blame, grabbed a trowel, smoothed out the tracks, and never said a word. Mitch, however, would never forget A.P.'s scowl, darkened and churned enough to drop a twister.

"Did you say 'troller'?"

"That's just the name Hollywood gives it." Mitch took his last swig and swung his bottle a little too far and clanked another empty one across the end table.

"When I heard 'troller,' all I could think of was maybe you'd hung a string a snoods on Mabry Lake. But the way you fish..."

"Basically, it's gettin' paid by *The Judge Smack Jack Show* for diggin' up dirt. Any kind a crazy-ass stories. Something unsolved, even filed lawsuits. Anything to make a case for his TV show. It's not the worst thing I've ever done."

A.P. laughed for a second and slapped both knees. "No, that would be when you lost my best pair a Channellocks."

"All this—drivin' through Scuffletown and seein' things. It stirred all of it. I don't think the whole story ever got told, to be straight up about it. I might could make something come out of Myron and Lori Leigh. Not sure what, though. If I was freelancin', it could be a movie."

"Don't forget"—A.P. yawned—"you been gone awhile. And since your family moved to Greenville, y'all ain't really considered Fountainville no more. You know how a small town does. It's likely some folks might not tell you nothin' about Lori Leigh and Myron. My guess is you gonna have to burn up some road tryin' to get some a these rocks to talk."

"Sometimes I can make 'em talk," Mitch said, and he realized that the beer was doing his talking.

"You might can, but don't forget…people ain't stopped weighin' in on that whole story. And I'm talkin' about all of it." A.P. stopped and took a long swig. "Ten years' worth is a lot a gossip gone under that bridge."

"Yeah, somethin' bad happens, and it's sooner or later got to have a cause or a blame. For some folks, havin' a blame gives 'em a way to deal with it," Mitch said and sank back into his chair.

A.P. startled Mitch out of a beer-buzz dream by cranking out of his chair. "Well, you ain't said it yet, but we all know…all roads lead to the Pink House," A.P. said. "Yep, Miss Sharona Riddle. She's got it all locked up in her head like some kind a nuclear code. You got to somehow find a way to get it out."

Mitch thought awhile about what A.P. said about Sharona Riddle and The Pink House. Mitch had always heard she was a sage, a fortune-teller, a poet, and even an ordained preacher. After a few minutes, he spotted a newspaper folded to the obituaries. "We ain't even talked about Billy yet."

"It's so much with all that." A.P. limped over to the newspaper and then dropped it into Mitch's lap.

"After Lori Leigh and Myron, I never knew what to say or do," Mitch said and stared down at the write-up on Billy Jeff Cole.

"That very next summer with y'all helpin', I remember watchin' you two best a friends since Little League baseball days, workin' side by side, and y'all were cuttin' some copper pipe," A.P. said.

"I think I remember that. Waitin' the whole time for Billy to somehow snap out of it."

"And not a word, not one damn thing between ya." A.P. popped his hands together.

Mitch didn't know how much further to push A.P., and it was close to midnight. "I'm takin' from readin' this, he died from some kind a cancer."

A.P. shook his head. "He fought as long as he could. They found it first in his liver, then the colon, and then in the bones, and that's when he went down fast."

"What did he ever say about Lori Leigh and Myron?" Mitch looked at his watch again.

A.P. stood up and moved toward the kitchen. "That sofa's a good sleeper. Lemme grab a pillow and a blanket." A.P. returned with his arms full, and Mitch wasn't sure if A.P. had heard his last question. "Later on...yeah, toward the end, he did. Let's save it for later." A.P. turned, threw up his hand, and skiffed his slippers back toward the other side of the house. "Oh, yeah. When you trollin', you do a lot a drivin'?"

"Let me just tell you the trollers' creed: if you troll, prepare to roll," Mitch said.

"Then you just hold on to that key," A.P. said as he closed his bedroom door.

With the lights snuffed out, Mitch bunched the cool covers under his chin and drifted into a symphony of frogs and cicadas joined in perfect time by the percussion of mayflies tapping at the window.

CHAPTER 10

The next morning, Mitch had already made it halfway up the handicap ramp of the Pink House before he realized that he had just walked all over Matthew, Mark, Luke, and John.

Painted gospel verses were splayed in cursive across the planks leading up to the house. At the end of the ramp, the back door behind the screen door stood wide open, and it unnerved him a bit to know how little space at that moment separated him from Sharona Riddle, the Pink House lady.

A quick scuff and then a flash appeared at the door, and he was startled by a skinny, caramel-skinned woman looking right back at him. She was in a New Orleans Saints jersey that she seemed to be wearing as a dress. Her hair was matted down with dozens of orange contraptions that from a distance looked more like a science-fair display of butterflies. "Whatchoo want, and can I help you with ya eyes gawkin' like all get-out?"

From farther back in the house, he heard another voice, slightly familiar and scratchy like an overplayed 45 record. "Sweetie? Sweetie? Who is it?" Mitch tried to see beyond the lady, who blocked most of the doorway, but he couldn't see a thing.

—

There's nothing like a certain tone of light or even an aroma to take you back to the memory of a place or time. A little swimmy-headed, but you're back. And Miss Sharona's interior lighting, a Blue Ribbon logo, and then the smell of what Mitch could only describe as spilled beer and ashtrays.

All of it had intermingled to transport him to his first transaction at the Pink House.

If you were under twenty-one, or if it was after Saturday midnight, South Carolina's blue laws slammed the door on purchasing any form of liquid that contained even a scintilla of alcohol. There were all kinds of cumbersome schemes available: underground deals made with liquor store employees after hours, persuading a stranger to make a purchase for a fee, and even fake IDs.

But sometimes you might just find yourself getting set up by an undercover cop or ratted out to your coach, Sunday school teacher, or worse, parents. But at the Pink House, especially for those under age, you always got bargain prices on quality beer and brand bourbons as well as the Pink House guarantee of anonymity.

Nobody knew how Sharona Riddle got away with it. And nobody much cared. Some people were convinced she had the power to heap a curse on someone. Other people claimed she had some dirt on Chief Swanger. The key was that she had to like you to trade with you, and you would have to convince her that a purchase was all for purposes of advancing a romance.

As Mitch distinctly remembered, his first time to the Pink House was a double date. Everybody got skittish about going inside and the ramifications of getting caught, and they dared him to do it. Once inside, he saw different sizes of crosses, a few candles, pictures of President Kennedy and Reverend King, and quilts draped over liquor boxes and Styrofoam coolers. He uncrumpled all his cash and pulled some pocket change. She kept calling him "sweetie times" as he struggled to count this change. All added up, he was fifty cents short of a six-pack. He remembered on the spot what Myron had told him to do. One, swear it was for courage because he was shy around girls. Two, if that didn't work, tell the Pink House lady he was friends with Myron. He followed Myron's formula, and Miss Sharona came alive, waving her arms, running her fingers across his cheek, and singing snippets of hymns. "Myron. Well, that Myron…he is my Congaree spider lily…a one and only." Even though he was fifty cents short, she went ahead and bagged up the full six-pack, but on several conditions: one, he had to promise to be a true gentleman, and two, he had to swear on a Bible to be in church on Sunday morning.

——

Mitch looked at the lady in the doorway. He only knew her as Sweetie. She slowly stretched her arm and locked the screen door, and then she pressed her whole body against the screen. "Pots an' pans? You dealin' pots an' pans? You best not be serving suit papers...'cause we ain't the ones. Go on. I got me a patient back there."

"I came to see my friend, Miss Sharona Riddle. I used to trade with her a while back. She might not remember me, but I know she'd know my late friend...Myron Parsons."

Mitch tried to interpret Sweetie's move as she put her hands on her hips and then patted her hair as if she were adjusting a crown.

"Myron Parsons? Ohhh...you the one, ain'tcha?" Sweetie looked over her shoulder. "Yeah, you the one's been askin' around. We been hearin' about you. And that Myron...yeah, Miss Sharona loved that boy." She lifted the latch, pushed the screen door, and pulled Mitch through by the elbow. She rambled on but in words he couldn't understand. She towed him through the kitchen and then down a passageway full of black-and-white photos of Miss Sharona posing with politicians and police officers. She stopped abruptly in front of a room with no light except a pair of neon beer signs, and there she was. The Pink House lady herself. Sprawled on a recliner, wearing a dark bathrobe, and cradling several loops of tubes. They led from her nose down to a tank flanked by gauges and wheels. Mitch waited reverently for her to speak.

"Well, step on over...lemme see that face full up." She squinted, tussled with the oxygen tubes, and moved in closer. Mitch breathed in a pleasant mixture of incense and Juicy Fruit.

"Miss Sharona?" Mitch tried his best to jump-start the conversation.

"Yeah, we traded somewhere along the way." She closed her eyes and looked back.

"Thank you for lettin' me come in. I know it's out a nowhere, and after so long."

"Oh, honey, I been knowin' you was comin'. That's what I told Sweetie when I woke up this very morning."

"Miss Sharona…" Sweetie interrupted and brought her a quilt. She palmed over five or six pills, different shapes and colors, and then presented her a glass of water. "You know he's the one's been askin' 'bout them suffocated teenagers. Whatchoo want me to do?"

"Lemme see what he needs…I can handle it…scoot on now."

"Miss Sharona…how you feelin'?" Mitch asked.

"I know that ain't why you here," she said. "You know small talk's for small walks."

Mitch felt a trickle of sweat inching down the middle of his spine.

"Do this new math for me, sir: nurse plus oxygen. That equals 'up against it.'"

"Miss Sharona, in all due respect, I been told by three people already if I wanna know all there is to know about it…Myron and Lori Leigh—"

She cut him off. "There we go. And truth wants to set you free." Miss Sharona's nose whistled as she raised her voice.

"They been tellin' me you're the one that knows the most." Mitch tried heaping some praise.

"They? You know what they say about crows? They all like the sound of other crows."

He knew he was in trouble. "Maybe I could come back some other time…could you let me make an appointment?" He held on, hoping for the best.

She inserted the tubes back into her nose. "You could. Problem is…I don't make appointments. That's for my God in heaven. And I can see, you all loaded up on questions. They's a time and place…lemme pray about it." The Pink House Lady dropped her head and went to sleep.

PART II

CHAPTER 11

September 20, 1970

On Friday, September 20, 1970, just before noon, Bud Culdock shut down his shoe shop, Culdock's Sole Music, for the day. Fountainville High had a home football game, and that always spiked the taxi business.

Culdock banked on a steady number of transports into town for an early-bird special, usually at Betty Jane's, for Barbecue Night. Then there were the trips to the stadium, followed shortly by more trips back home if either the weather turned bad or the score got out of hand. That day he opted to drive his taxi home for an exterior and interior cleaning.

When he pulled up, a black Lincoln Continental with dealer tags had parked squarely on top of the area reserved for washing.

He stepped up to the porch and jiggled a double-bolted front door.

As the door eased open, a naked man holding a fireplace poker in one hand and a wad of clothes in the other leaped from the bedroom, tangled his legs, and tripped headfirst into the kitchen. Bud was standing next to the cabinet where he always kept a loaded .38. His shaking hands struggled with getting the drawer open, and then he grabbed the gun and stalked toward the kitchen. As soon as he took his first step inside, a man hacked his free arm with the poker.

Culdock fell over to one side and fired at the same time. The bullet struck the intruder in the torso, and from his knees Culdock watched the man fall face first and then claw the floor, leaving a bloody trail toward the back door. The wounded man moved only a few feet on the linoleum floor and never turned over to show his face. When the naked man totally stopped moving, Bud ran to the bedroom and found his wife scrambling to find her clothes. When she yelled "You loser son of a bitch," Bud Culdock instinctively swung the pistol around and fired another shot at her, but the bullet sailed just past her head and lodged in the sheetrock inches from their wedding picture.

———

In the months that followed, Bud Culdock was charged with, tried for, and then acquitted of voluntary manslaughter for the death of Dee Gray. The defense counsel, Hamlet Mabry, known for his wily and compelling closing arguments, successfully convinced the jury that it was a case of self-defense. The disappointed assistant solicitor who prosecuted the case against Culdock blamed the not-guilty verdict on the whole town of Fountainville. He explained at his posttrial news conference that Fountainville was one of those rare pockets of demographics where a snake-tongued defense lawyer could successfully employ the "he just needed killing" defense and win a man's acquittal for homicide.

Gray had been a county councilman and car dealership owner from Greenville. Bud's wife, Rhonda Sparks-Culdock, was Gray's personal secretary. After her husband's trial, she reluctantly relented to the solicitor's pleas to consent to the state's dismissal of the attempted murder charge that she had pressed against her husband. The solicitor's ace in the hole was a charge against her for shoplifting that cropped up days after her husband's trial ended.

Within a month of Bud Culdock's not-guilty verdict and the final order granting the final divorce, Rhonda Sparks-Culdock departed Fountainville for the last time.

The last word Bud heard about her was that she had dropped her married name and taken a job managing a business called the Golden Dolphin, a combo strip club and pancake house on the outskirts of Myrtle Beach.

—

In the wake of years following the shooting of Dee Gray, the community of Fountainville felt part sympathy and pity for Bud Culdock, but the weight of the scandal darkened Chicago Cabs with an unrelenting shadow of uncertainty. People were willing to drop their shoes off at Culdock's shoe shop, Sole Music, and just as quickly depart, but calls to Culdock's side taxi business dwindled to next to nothing. After several years passed, taxi calls eventually began to slowly increase, but that would change when Culdock discovered a smoking GTO and two dead teenagers.

CHAPTER 12

For the rest of the afternoon following the Mitch Beam encounter, Sharona Riddle and Sweetie Bates talked about the snippets of Miss Sharona's dream from the night before. The one that warned about a trader from the past. Their conversation interweaved with spells of watching Miss Sharona's favorite daytime stories, *Days of Our Lives* and *Another World*. "You don't trifle with a premonition." Sharona repeated a few times until her voice shifted poorly to the next gear.

Sweetie scribbled on the patient chart. Miss Sharona's blood-pressure numbers had escalated. "Old lady, you ain't got no business talkin' to a livin' soul unless you just *have* to."

"Sweetie, we woke up this morning, and we was still part a something, some kind a mission, but from here on, it's gonna be a thorn in the flesh."

Sweetie crossed her arms. "So…more prayin'?"

"Sweetie cakes…you guessed right. We 'bout to get down on some real prayin' now. And here's what I'm sayin'…moanin' and whinin' prayin' ain't real prayin'. We got us a fight on our hands with Satan hisself. So it's pure knees-on-the-floor prayin' from here on out."

"Now listen here." Sweetie picked up an insulin syringe. "Don't getcha sugars all worked up again. I can't have you flyin' to glory. Not on my shift. No, ma'am."

Miss Sharona was quiet for a bit, as if she were already praying. "Sweetie, is that Mitch Beam friend or foe? Satan'll take on all kinds a shapes." She settled down, but when Sweetie didn't answer, her anger percolated one more time. "You know, in just the right twist of air or slant of light, even a turkey buzzard looks like a hawk."

"Preach it, patient lady." Sweetie kept her going.

"All this comin' up again about Myron...I tell you what I *can* do. I can put it behind me. Thought I done did that. I can do it again. Get behind me, Satan." Miss Sharona got real quiet and folded her hands underneath her chin.

CHAPTER 13

After the hour-and-a-half encounter with Sharona Riddle, Mitch began to doubt any prospects coming out of the convoluted Lori Leigh and Myron story. The pressure of coming up with something for *The Judge Smack Jack Show* was also intensifying on his cash flow.

He made a McDonald's stop and drove to the Fountainville magistrate's court to take a peek at their civil case filings. He whipped his Cutlass into the drive from the main highway and barely avoided a rear-ender from what looked like Bud Culdock's taxi. It went by way too fast to tell. He slid slightly on a patch of gravel, slowed, and then eased into a mostly empty lot. When he parked, he noticed a regiment of Leyland cypresses that loomed along a bank behind the building. Three of them together had died and turned fox orange and looked stark among the other green ones.

The woman's voice dropped on him as soon as the door closed. "Judge ain't in, sir…how can I help ya?"

Mitch didn't see the woman at first. "Just need to see the new civil suits."

The hidden lady said she thought he looked like he might be a landlord. She told him he had a scowl, and she figured he just wanted to sue the hell out of somebody. She said she had a firecracker little sister who sometimes got that look on her face.

"Ma'am…wherever you are…I'm a case finder. It's like this. You ever watch *The Judge Smack Jack Show*? I'm workin' for them."

A petite lady wearing platform shoes and holding a broom like a shotgun shot out from a row of file cabinets. He didn't see or hear her approach.

She adjusted a rogue clump of gray hair that had slid down below an obvious black wig. "What type a case?" she asked.

"I need what you might call a flaming bobby dazzler. Something good for TV."

She let the broom handle clank against a trash can and pointed to a file cabinet in the far corner. "Go on and have at it…but you ain't got but ten minutes to do it by my watch. We got permission to shut down early. So, come hell or high water."

He wasted no time getting to the file cabinet and digging in. Opening the first drawer gave off an unmistakable smell of smoke and mowed grass. "You the clerk of court?"

The lady's responsive snicker unfolded like a celery crunch. "Not officially. But I pretty much do it, so you could say that. I'm Kathy Moss. Fountainville born and raised. You know, you look like somebody. Maybe somebody I used to know."

"Name's Mitch. Mitch Beam. My family's from here, or they used to be, anyway. I went to Fountainville High…class a seventy-seven." He looked up, and she was gone.

"I'm security too, in case you didn't notice. You're not supposed to see me anyway. And by the ways, did my bell go off when you came in? I'm testin' her out. By the way, while you looking, our newest filings are in the bottom drawer. Oldest in the top drawer. So I'm keeping tabs, and you're down to three and a half on my watch."

"It sure would be a time-saver if you could point out something that's worth a hoot. Maybe something wild and scandalous."

"Yes, I guess I'm the only one that could. Might be of mutual benefit in a way. Kill two birds," she said. "Tell you what. Look up Peterson versus Burden. Pretty sure that was the one…see it?"

"Here we go." Mitch snapped up the file, and the drawer clunked back into place.

"Here's the gist of it," she said with a lower Greenville County accent so that "gist" consisted of about three and a half syllables. Miss Moss went on to tell him that she referred to the Peterson case as the "Soothsayer versus Mr. Speedo." She told him that she was working the intake desk when the plaintiff came in and then told her the whole story. The plaintiff lady had a German shepherd, and the defendant, who was always having wild pool parties with large groups of men all wearing Speedos, had two poodles. She said they were the little prissy kind and not the big kind. She said the plaintiff lady called them "toy" poodles. And the way it happened was there was this big chain-link fence, and one night those toy poodles dug a hole under the fence and just bit the hell out of her German shepherd. Miss Moss then said that the plaintiff lady listed her occupation as "soothsayer."

Mitch was beginning to think there was nothing to it until he heard "soothsayer." He asked her to tell him some more.

And Miss Moss said she would, but he was about to run out of time. She paused and picked up where she left off. She said the defendant came in about three weeks after the soothsayer lady filed her suit, and he was pretty much what she had suspected. A little light in his loafers. And then she said the defendant man dropped two bombshells. One, he told her that the plaintiff lady slept in a coffin on her back screen porch. And he asked, "So why couldn't she hear all the commotion and stop it?" And then she said that the man came up with a right refined analysis and defense that he included in his answer. Miss Moss said that the second bombshell was the defense that there was no way it could have been foreseeable to him—specifically, all that his poodles would do. And then Miss Moss said that was where it got right impressive, intellectually.

She said Mr. Speedo's defense was that since the plaintiff was a soothsayer and a professional in the fortune-telling trade, if she couldn't predict what was going to happen, then why should *he*, a mere lay person, be expected to foresee it?

"Well, well, well, Miss Moss, that's what I'm talkin' about," Mitch said.

"And it's startin' to come back to me…I think you were in school with my baby sister."

"Who's that?" Mitch asked while he was flipping through the Peterson complaint.

"I'm Kathy Moss…well, really, I used to be a Stone. I'm Amelia's sister. Now she's just Lady A. So we're a couple a rollin' stones. That's who we are. Small world."

Mitch twisted to see where she was. He couldn't find her, but he asked anyway. "Amelia Stone? She's your sister? She was friends with Lori Leigh Cole?" he asked.

"*Best* friends…the very best. Law have mercy, that was some kind a deal. All that mess with Myron's car and all. And then along comes the strange and sorry life of Billy Cole, Lori Leigh's brother…you heard about Billy, right?"

"Oh, yes, ma'am. That's why I'm back in town. Your sister. She still around?"

"By the way," Miss Moss said, returning from around a row of file cabinets, "you down to thirty-two seconds on my watch, so whatcha gonna do? But yeah, since you asked me, she's here. She owns this highfalutin dress shop out on Woodruff Road. I mean to tell you, they serve beer and wine, the whole deal. And even though she's Baptist, she gets by with it. Whatcha think about that?"

"May I go ahead and get me a copy of that file?"

"No, sir, you surely *cannot*. Your time is flat out. And I'm lockin' up. But if you was to come back tomorrow, I'll have it then. Already copied and organized. I'm a turnkey operation, sir."

CHAPTER 14

When Mitch got to A.P.'s that evening, the whole house smelled of bacon and burnt loaf bread. Steam rose and flattened out above a stack of pancakes, a platter of grits, and a mound of Valleydale bacon. When Mitch stepped into the kitchen, A.P. was singing Jerry Lee Lewis songs and had his back turned, spooning up the scrambled eggs. The coffee percolator babbled in perfect rhythm.

"A.P., it's a Waffle House in here," Mitch said and looked around for something he could do to help.

"While you up, pour that coffee. Don't worry if it's still perking. It's close enough to bein' done. My timing's never quite right."

Mitch brought two cups to the table and started telling A.P. about the day even before they could sit. "I took your advice, boss. Got up my nerve and went around to the Pink House. I broke the ice. Tried to anyway. But that Miss Sharona, she's a hard one."

"How'd she look?" A.P. asked and proceeded to mix his grits into his scrambled eggs. "I heard she's lookin' rough. Death's door."

"She was using oxygen. I saw that. And she had a nurse. Mean as a cornered possum. Seemed like...Miss Sharona's thinking was fine. And she's still feisty," Mitch said.

"Well," A.P. said, "I been stewin' on it, just like you told me. I tell you somebody else that could fill in some blanks if you could trust him. But you can't...Cat Swanger." A.P. took a few bites and sipped his coffee.

"Fill me in," Mitch said.

"Back when Lori Leigh and Myron died," A.P. said, "he was just plain deputy. But he's *Chief* Swanger now. Cat had a well-known hate-on for Myron. Always tellin' tales about Myron cuttin' doughnuts on the golf course, spray-paintin' street signs. That was Cat's biggest beef. Whenever he uttered Myron's name, 'vandal' was the caboose right behind that engine. Cat wouldn't let it go."

"That don't sound like Myron," Mitch said. "Swanger ever catch him at it?"

"Hell no…and then there's somebody else too: Duvy Skelton. The old golf pro down at the Whip-Poor-Will Golf Course. But he's long gone… moved or got run out. Prob'ly shot dead by now. He claimed that Myron stole golf balls out the water hazards at the golf course. The whole town a Fountainville laughed at both of 'em. Behind their backs, of course. Yeah, those two guys got to be right tight." A.P. got up and poured another coffee.

"My ex told me one time…" A.P. leaned forward. "She said she had a radar for it…she said Cat was kind a sweet on Miss Lori Leigh. But she was always sayin' shit like that. Nothin' but a pot stirrer."

Mitch let all that sink in for a bit. "A.P., that ain't no bombshell. That ain't a bit a nothin'. Who didn't have a crush on Lori Leigh Cole? Nope, that ain't nothin' to that."

The two of them sat and sipped coffee for a while until a stack of dishes and pans shifted in the sink and broke the spell.

"You know what? I'm glad as hell you got my message about Billy and come back up here," A.P. said. "Nice just to catch up."

"I'm just glad you didn't forget me." Mitch thought for a second. "I'm beginnin' to learn what the term 'hell on earth' means. I think it means when people don't remember you anymore."

"You might have something there," A.P. said.

Mitch remembered his meeting that day with Kathy Moss. "I think I found me a case. Met a lady named Kathy Moss down at the magistrate's court. Then I found out she's Amelia Stone's sister. She helped me break my slump. This case might just do it. But goin' back to all that sign business with Myron. Cuttin' doughnuts and all that sign paintin'. That don't sound a bit like Myron. That's bullshit."

"Yeah," A.P. said. "Yeah, I know. Now tell me about that Kathy Moss case."

CHAPTER 15

"Myron Parsons…ol' Myron…man, whatchoo talkin' about?" Rusha Goldsmith said right off the bat. He waved Mitch Beam into a booth at Betty Jane's Diner. "Now, tell me flat out: Why you so wantin' to get that all stirred up?"

"To keep my lights on, for one thing," Mitch said, and he quickly pushed his clutch and coasted for a few seconds. Mitch went on to describe for Rusha that he worked for the *Judge Smack Show*, and he told him what a troller was. He told him that he was staying with A.P. and that he was going to see if he could find some stories and cases for the show. Then he said that he and A.P. had been talking one night, and he started thinking about Myron and Lori Leigh, and maybe there was a story there, especially since it seemed so unsettled about what really happened. It seemed like Rusha might be a fertile source.

"I could say some things…yeah, I could," Rusha said.

"I'm tryin' to learn all I can about it, Rusha. How it all happened. So, for starters, what about 'carbon monoxide'? You buyin' that?" Mitch asked.

"I heard that." Rusha pulled a napkin out of the dispenser and dabbed his face a few times. "Yeah, I heard all that about carbon monoxide. I don't know why this just now jumped in my head, but you know that golf pro? Duvy Skelton? Except we always said 'Skel-uh-ton' right to his face. One time, though, whoo-ee. Once he caught me and Myron swimmin' for golf balls. In that old pond right in front the thirteenth green. You know the way that fairway swoops right into it. We were in that pond carryin' on, and Skel-uh-ton sneaked up on us. One a them electric carts was how. And he called us all kind a shit. Then he said Myron ought not be swimmin' with *my* kind. Pissed us both off. Myron's whole thing anyway was to get them balls to the junior golfers. Help 'em out. But Skel-uh-ton took every last one of 'em. Every damn one. And then he up and sold all them balls in the pro shop. Put all that money in *his* pocket."

"That pro ever go to Swanger with it?" Mitch asked.

"That might a been a while before Skel-uh-ton and Swanger got to be so tight. Yeah…way before Myron and Lori Leigh got found by the shoe-shop man. That sure would a been fuel to the fire if he had," Rusha said and threw out his hands. "Woosh. But don't worry. We took care a that golf-ball thing. Yes we did."

—

July 1975

At dusk, a garden-variety thunderstorm appeared to be about an hour or two away. Sheet lightning shook loose occasional bursts of blue-green light below, and a slight breeze whipped up whispers among the bumping cattails and the stalks of a nearby bamboo stand.

Rusha Goldsmith stood lookout while Myron Parsons unbuckled, hopped on one leg a few times, and then slipped off his yellow double-knits. Rusha watched Myron regain his balance, line up his shoes, and hang his shirt and pants on a utility guy-wire that disappeared into the weeds. In his boxer shorts, he scrabbled along the grassy bank beside Peters Creek, the main water hazard that ran through the Whip-Poor-Will Golf Course.

Rusha unsnapped his overalls and kicked off a pair of faded high-tops. The soles were crayon green from walking on so much golf-course grass. The tips were held together by staples and electrical tape. Rusha could see that his skin helped him become part of the night, but the jockey underwear was as stark as a neon beer sign.

Rusha made his way toward Myron until they stood next to each other on the bank. He elbowed around Myron and aimed his flashlight below toward the water. They both made choppy steps to get closer to the tumbling creek sounds. Rusha reached into the water and ran his hands along the chicken-wire trap they had stretched across the creek a week earlier. They had used the shafts of broken golf clubs to stake each end of their trap and hold it in place.

After several swipes, Rusha scooped out over fifty glistening golf balls. He tossed each one to Myron, who plunked them into a duffel bag one by one.

On the return, they scampered back across the creek, and then they stopped to shine the flashlight onto Golf Pro Skelton's golf-ball trap set up farther downstream. It was completely empty, and the water almost seemed to snicker as it sieved through Skelton's box of dispirited chicken wire and door flaps.

CHAPTER 16

The next morning before sunrise, Mitch threw together a couple of boiled eggs and a toasted slice of Bunny Bread. He left a perking coffeepot for A.P., who said he had plans to rough in a house near Simpson Inn, and if the heat held off, he'd go ahead and load in a cast-iron tub.

About an hour later, Mitch drove through Scuffletown past Tornado Alley, where contorted hollies and a trail of stumps still left a conspicuous scar.

—

On successive spring nights in 1973, possibly as many as three tornadoes cut swaths of trees with roots completely out of the ground, tossed structures and equipment, and even dug a ten-foot-wide trench that lacerated Scuffletown Road near the dance barn. No fatalities, except if you count a shed full of peacocks and laying hens. And no one saw or photographed any of the funnel clouds. In the following days, government officials disputed from the get-go that any bona fide twisters touched down. A US Weather Bureau spokesman declared that it was just a series of "wind shears" that caused all the damage.

Over the next eight months, Mayor Leon Forrest offered assorted excuses to explain his failure to conjure up any federal storm relief money for the town. As a result, Fountainville rode him out on a rail in the next election. In the mayor's concession speech, he boo-hooed a couple of times, and at the very end, he referred to his lopsided defeat as "the *real* tragedy." The next day's postelection headline in the *Tribune Gazette* declared, "Twister Returns to Wipe Out Forrest."

—

Later that morning, Mitch found himself standing in front of the store-front windows of Lady A's Petites. They glinted sharply as they clashed with the first of the morning sun.

Mitch saw the proprietress, Amelia Stone, known to most as Lady A. She glided into the main showroom. Her hands were wrapped around a teacup that left a tiny steam trail. He noticed that as she neared the front window, she seemed to bounce the sun's prism light in skewed directions.

Lady A was known to believe in omens and signs, even ghosts. She once gave her personal testimony at Rocky Creek Baptist Church in which she interweaved tales of what she called her "encounters" with the ghost of Benjamin Franklin Stairley and even her late best friend, Lori Leigh Cole. The Wednesday Night Encouragers Class quietly took measures to remove her from the speakers list.

—

Just as she finished pulling back the remaining swatch of curtains, Mitch moved in closer to the glass and lost track of her as she moved to the back again. He remembered what A.P. told him when her name came up. "Just watch ya step. She's a looker. You'll see what I mean. But...she bears watchin'."

"Seems I've been waiting my whole life to talk to a girl looks like that," Mitch thought, trying to will himself to move forward. He gradually fell prey to the more comforting tug telling him that it would be best to come back at another time. He turned and looked across the cloud-winnowed tree lines and rolling hills leading back toward Scuffletown, hating what-ever it was that made him reluctant to enter Lady A's. He walked back, got into his car, and began the return trip to Fountainville to retrieve the Soothsayer/Mr. Speedo file from Kathy Moss.

CHAPTER 17

"**I** guess I pretty much saved your heinie," the voice of Kathy Moss fire-crackered out of nowhere and went silent just as abruptly. The bell above the door prinkled steadily down to a whisper. "I barely can hear that bell…it still ain't cuttin' it."

Mitch couldn't discern where her voice came from, but he got clues every few seconds from a whap and a muffled "shit fire" or two. Several seconds snailed by awkwardly, and without any warning, Kathy emerged wearing goggles and oversized garden gloves. She could have been mistaken for a tall-ship swashbuckler, twirling and presenting her metal flyswatter to invading pirates.

"You can't put serious money on timer sprays. And when it comes to these big-uns, you might as well inflict the death penalty all by yourself. Just take things into your own hands."

"Madame Clerk, did you by chance copy that Soothsayer/Speedo file for me?"

"I was, and I did, and you just missed all the drama that busted out close to ten minutes ago. First thing, one of your own kind, from one of them other judge shows, they just walked in and immediately bird-dogged it. CBS, I think they said they were. That's when I had to go full Rahab on 'em. I said I had an official hold on that file. And then I told them that somebody had beat 'em to the punch yesterday. I don't even know if I had authority to say that. Let's just say they were less than pleased. But then I helped 'em find another one. Put 'em onto the scent of other game. They seemed somewhat satisfied, so it's a win-win."

"Well, I owe ya, Miss Moss."

"Hear this. If you can't lie for a friend, who can you lie for? " Miss Moss cocked her head and cleared her throat. "So…what's goin' on with you and the Pink House?"

The question surprised Mitch. He felt his face growing warmer. "Oh… me and Miss Sharona? Well, we caught up a little bit."

"Whatever it was you got caught up on…must not a set too well to Miss Sharona's way a thinkin'," said Miss Moss.

"So how do you know all that, if you don't mind tellin'?" Mitch asked.

"Her caretaker stomped down here askin' for Chief Swanger. The part I heard was Miss Sharona's all upset with your 'terragation.' That's what she kept callin' it."

"I just tried to ask her a little bit a what she knew about Myron and Lori Leigh," Mitch said. "That's all I did."

"Yep…she said somethin' about that too," Kathy Moss said. "From what I heard, she wanted to know what she could do to stop you. Legal-wise, I mean."

"I heard she's always been known as the town sage…" Mitch said.

"Yeah. And they say every town's got at least one, but somethin' else you should know, especially in your line a work. Miss Sharona and Chief Swanger's close. Been real close a long time. They share information. She's been his eyes and ears. And in return, he just looked the other way on all her tradin'. Take it from me, you best keep your powder dry."

"And, how about Lady A's? You go round there yet?"

"I just did a little bit ago. Didn't see a soul. I might go by again later."

"Oh, she's already called and told me all about that. She said, 'Guess who I just think I saw standin' outside my store?' She thought it was you. And she kept askin' why you didn't come in."

Mitch swiped the sweat off his lip and cheeks. "She said all that? Well…I might could go around there."

As he walked out, file in hand, he looked back one more time and caught Kathy Moss making a backhanded swing to coldcock a fly in mid-flight. She gathered it up with a coffee cup and flipped it into the trashcan.

CHAPTER 18

August 10, 1975

The phone call jolted Jimmy Fonda out of a restless sleep full of dream fragments. It came just seconds before the tweeps of the seven o'clock alarm shut down any chance for any more sleep. He reached for the alarm clock first, but his right arm got twisted in the sheets, which handcuffed him. He opted to swing his left arm and roll to grab the receiver. He strained to hear Cat Swanger's voice over the alarm, and all he heard him say was something about he was using the phone at Gilreath Farms. Then he said something else about "Scuffletown Road" and "near the Gilder Creek Bridge," and then a much more emphatic "You get the hell down here."

His sweaty palms slipped a little on his Harley handle grips. He got onto Scuffletown Road within minutes, and he soon passed Waylon Riggins's customized ice cream truck ambulance moving along sluggishly. Its red and white lights tumbled, but there was no siren.

Since he was closing in on the Vaughn Farm's obscured driveway, he figured maybe Old Man Vaughn's ticker had finally shut down and caused him to run across the road and hit a tree or a cow, or worse, somebody's bull.

At the bottom of the steepest hill near Gilreath Farms, Jimmy saw a cloud of smoke, a collection of flashing lights, Cat Swanger's squad car, a tow truck, and even Bud Culdock's taxi. He eased his motorcycle over onto the grassy shoulder so that it was nose to nose with Cat's car. From there he saw what looked to be a swarm of blue and gray uniforms. Some were standing. Others were bent over or squatting and looking under and around what looked like Myron Parsons's GTO. But there was no sign of any other vehicle. No metal or busted glass in the roadway.

Cat Swanger's head popped up from behind the lid of the GTO's trunk. His face was a spring tomato on the verge of reaching summer red. Easing up from a squat-down position, he swiped his cheek sweat with both hands and then limped a few times from side to side. As Swanger crossed the road, he hitched his pants up and teetered as if he were wading over river rock, looking for a better spot to cast a fly.

"Jimbo, we got us some bad shit. Real bad. You know whose car that is...hell, who don't? Before I walk you down there, I got to ask...Was you the one that did Myron's muffler work?"

Jimmy saw that Cat wasn't looking him in the face. He did recall talking to Myron a couple weeks earlier about the exhaust system. Basically trouble-shooting for him. He knew he hadn't touched that vehicle. "He came by. I took a peek. We talked. That was it. I told him he had a couple a holes, looked like. Maybe rusted out. And that he probably needed to replace his piping. He asked me what a catalytic converter was, and I recommended one because it wasn't standard on a sixty-five GTO. He said thanks. That was it." Jimmy was puzzled about Swanger's muffler-work question.

Jimmy waited for Cat to respond, and he watched him turn back toward the GTO. The tree shadows were as faint as sketch strokes as they fell across the haze enveloping the car. One of the deputy coroners opened the back door, reached down into a Styrofoam cooler, and pulled out two six-packs of beer bottles, all of them capped and dripping water.

"Y'all leave that...leave it the hell right where it is." Cat Swanger's voice startled them into dropping and clanking both six-packs back into the cooler.

"Anybody else hear what y'all talked about?" Swanger asked.

"It was just us. And Chief, you know Myron. He's the only one that ever touched his baby...he okay?"

"Okay? He's damn dead, man. Lori Leigh's gone too. And you won't believe who found 'em: Culdock and his half-ass taxi. Can you believe I got to somehow explain that shit?"

Cat Swanger took a couple of steps and leaned in so close that his lips almost touched Jimmy's ear. "Okay...I can say I saw y'all talkin' that day—just talkin', no work. And not one damn thing about discussing those rusty parts or holes or a catalytic whatever you said you might a seen. Myron always did his own work. Stick to that. I'll back that up."

"I did start to tell him to drive with the windows down, just in case... until he was able to fix it. But Myron always drove with 'em down. So I never did say nothin' about that," Jimmy mumbled. His hands began to sweat.

Swanger pulled away and looked at him once more, this time square on but shaking. "You don't wanna get your ass sued off, do ya? Ya damn right. Stick to what we said if anybody asks you about it. Now walk over there and tell me what ya see."

When the trooper directing cars turned to stop a growing line of traffic, Jimmy tucked his head and shot across the road. Swanger's words about Myron and Lori Leigh made his knees wobbly. He took stuttered steps toward the GTO. All the windows were closed, and a faint layer of smudge had formed inside the glass. He was pleased that there were no bodies inside. Even though the engine had stopped, he heard the faint sound of a song still crackling on the radio, as if it was partly on and off the station.

He pictured what he could remember about Myron and Lori Leigh, and he could see them cruising with their hair flared back. Both singing with the music blasting. Myron with one arm around his girl, and the other one could have been a bunting slung over the top of the door frame. Yeah, Myron loved driving with his windows down. Always had those windows down. "No need to tell him to do that," he said to himself and looked around to see if anyone was close enough to hear.

He hesitated to move any farther because of the blockade of three of four troopers and even the tow-truck driver, Hooks Hammond. They were whispering and crouching at the back of the car. They seemed to be pushing limbs and high grass away from the bumper. Somebody said something about "weeds in the muffler." He glanced into the backseat of the GTO. There was a magazine cover with the heading BELMONT UNIVERSITY. Several pages were torn and strewn across the seat.

Cat Swanger huddled up with another group of men including the coroner. When Swanger turned his back, Jimmy Fonda eased across the road again. He rolled his cycle for about fifty yards and then cranked it as quietly as he could and drove straight to his muffler shop.

Jimmy's bike tires crunched the driveway gravel just short of eight thirty that morning, a good thirty seconds or so behind the arrival of the Harley growl. No helmet, flip-flops several sizes too small. Overgrown toenails. His ponytail was a cinnamon roll twirled and clipped at the nape of his neck.

He stayed on the bike long enough for the dust and exhaust to blow across the roof of the shop. His hands and arms were shaking too much to get the key in the lock or to hold a pen when he got inside.

—

Jimmy survived two stints as a rescue helicopter pilot in Vietnam, or what he liked to call "the war against my cousin Jane." He was never much for detail about the war, and the most anybody could ever squeeze out of him was "Yeah, that was a doozie all right," or "it was some kind a shit." He would just walk away if somebody ever pushed him on it.

In 1974, at the end of his last tour of duty, he returned to his family in Fountainville, and for the first few months, he never said much except to complain about things, like Nixon or the price of beer and gas. He went prematurely gray, and his facial hair filled in like a neglected collard patch. Out of nowhere he began to talk about his dream of owning a muffler shop, and that idea landed like head lice on his family, made up mostly of medical professionals.

The whole family was surprised that Jimmy had any knowledge of mechanics, engines, or exhaust systems, and they surmised that he learned it in the military. His dad had plans for him to take over the two-genera- tion family optometry practice, Fonda's Frames. Their logo featured a wolf wearing a nightgown and cap as well as a giant pair of spectacles. "Better to see you with" was in the sentence bubble just above the wolf's snout.

It took Jimmy about two months to fabricate a two-stall concrete block garage on the lowest-lying portion of the family land fronting on Main Street. Granddaddy Fonda had a small spell about the way the garage stalls opened up to face Main Street, so Jimmy extended and looped the driveway so that cars could feed into the stalls at the back of the building. He didn't say anything about Jimmy's sign: Jimmy Fonda Mufflers—We're Fonda Your Business.

—

Jimmy couldn't get his mind off the smell that was out there surrounding Myron's car. A blend of a cigar, radiator fluid, and a touch of burning grass. Kind of like his granddaddy's den, which was used for smoking stogies, sipping liquor, reading the Bible, and Thursday-night poker.

He jiggled the key until the door gave in, and he stood on the threshold for a few minutes. He found some blank paper to write on and stuck his notes into the middle of a stack of documents spread out on the To Be Filed tray.

CHAPTER 19

Lady A was best known for her country good looks, her spiritual gift of hospitality, and especially for her quarterly Season Pleazins. Every spring, summer, fall, and winter, she would stage elaborate rollouts of trending clothing lines and accessories.

When customers and their spouses or significant others entered the shop during Season Pleazins Week, Lady A would personally escort the men toward the back of the store and her setup of a fully stocked bar complete with short-skirted female bartenders. In order to ensure a wink and a nod from Chief Swanger over the unlicensed sales of alcohol, she was instructed by the chief to handwrite "complimentary liquid snacks in honor of local churches" at the bottom of the clothing receipts.

As the female customers shopped and made their rack-selection stacks for the dressing rooms, the tight wallet fortifications of the hapless men crumbled like the walls of Jericho.

—

Mitch succumbed to Kathy Moss's cajoling, and he returned to Lady A's Petites later that afternoon. Before entering, he stopped to admire the fluorescent Season Pleazins plane banner. Even when rolled up, it looked larger than necessary and filled up the entire length of the glass storefront. When he saw Lady A, his throat instantly parched and closed. He began to sweat. The same phenomenon had occurred years before whenever he was in the proximity of either Lori Leigh Cole or Lady A.

Lady A's ensemble was a pair of tight white pedal pushers, lavender platform sandals with leather string straps that crisscrossed up each leg, a multicolored scarf-belt, and a lime-green silk blouse knotted on one side to show a hint of her tanned hip curve. On her, the rig-out somehow harmonized. She stood barely as high as her clothes racks, even in platforms, and she appeared as light and bouncy as a bouquet of Shasta daisies.

She had her front door customized with a doorbell that belted out a few lines from her favorite tunes. He entered at three o'clock and triggered "Hit me with ya best shot…fy-yer away-hay…" booming from the ceiling.

All his rehearsed lines began to scramble between his brain and tongue like colliding freight trains. His entire face felt as if it had locked into a permanent smile just as soon as she spoke.

"Well, helllll-oh, Mitch Beam. Have your ears been burning?"

"Hello, Miss Amelia…or do you prefer Lady A?"

"Either one. You know I saw you out there this morning when I opened up. I get going errr-ly, friend. Work comes easy for those who love their work. Do you love what you do? *The Judge Smack Jack Show*, right?" she asked and winked.

"You knew that?"

"My sister Kathy…and some others…told me."

"Your sister's a nice lady. She might a helped put some money in my pocket. Found me a case to use *and* copied the whole thing for me. She said she was turnkey, and she was right. Nice lady. And she was braggin' on you and your shop. I see why."

"You are still so cute and sweet…just like when you and Billy used to hang out. You and those goo-goo eyes for Lori Leigh. My sweet dear friend. Best friend I ever had…or ever will, I suppose. And then Billy. Bless his poor soul. He never was the same. Suffered so. I heard you made it to the funeral."

Mitch saw that she looked like she was about to cry, and he didn't know what to do or say. He feared some waterworks. He instinctively reached for a nearby table and pretended to be captivated by a display of earrings and bracelets, but it turned out to be a false alarm.

"Nice stuff you got here," he managed to get out.

"There you go again, Mr. Sweet-Feet. Hold on. I gotta go in the back and put my boobs on. Oops, I prob'ly shouldn't a said that. But oh well. Hold on."

Mitch admired the way she walked. It was as if she were on rails. She snapped the dressing room curtain and never stopped talking.

"So, Mitch Beam…what were you doing at the Pink House?"

Her question caught him off guard. "A.P.…A.P.'s the one made me do it. He said it made sense to go to Miss Sharona. How'd you know about that?"

"Well, what for? I heard She's right sick. She don't trade in her liquid arts anymore." Lady A giggled.

"A.P. says she's the one person who just knows stuff, like she's some kind of female prophet. Even writes poems," he said.

"She is some kind of a medium. Yeah, I've heard that."

"I got to thinkin' about Lori Leigh and Myron. That whole thing. You think somebody could make a TV show out of it?" He didn't have any feel for how Lady A would react. The long pause agitated him into speaking up again. "I'd at least like to pick her brain. Maybe yours too."

"Well…you know Fountainville," she said. "You remember how news starts and then flows in and out."

"Yep…flows and flows," he said.

"You mean we might could get some publicity? This old town?" she asked.

"Potentially, I guess. First, I got to dig around. Come up with some kind a angle. Then, if I come up with something, I have to convince all my bosses and producers."

"Now…me and Lori Leigh." She paused. "Let's see if I can say *any-*thing about it without turning into a tear-and-snot machine."

"If you have time to catch up," he said.

"Lemme ask my girls about my afternoon showings. I think most a my regulars are holdin' back for my upcoming Season Pleazins. Just around the corner. If I get to goin' on, I'll have trouble bringin' it in for a landin'."

She sailed away again, leaving a perfumed waft that settled gently upon him. In a few moments the fragrance welled up more thoughts of Lori

Leigh, and one of her songs in particular. "Once in a Lifetime." She sang it in the musical *Stop the World—I Want to Get Off.* He never forgot the song or every word of the play title.

Lady A dropped back in on him like a late-afternoon pop-up shower with the sun still shining. "I got a customer set for four o'clock, Mitch Beam. Could you come back around five thirtyish?"

"That'll work," he told her. On his return trip through the lot and to his car, he thought, "Right there's a cloud with no rain. A pretty cloud. But no rain."

CHAPTER 20

Mitch returned just as planned to Lady A's Petites just a few minutes before five o'clock, and he set off the door chime again. This time it was the Roy Orbison classic "Pretty Woman." The chime played one line and cut off in the middle of the next one. He saw Lady A and one of her assistants tending to a customer whose arm stretched out from a dressing room and snatched a handful of clothes. Lady A was barefoot and flitting from one clothes rack to another. She hooked two hangers to the back of her blouse collar, squeezed pins and tags between her lips, and looped a pair of pants on one arm and two pocketbooks on the other.

The dressing room lady coughed and flung a hanger against the dressing room wall. "Amelia, honey…no, uh, no, this stuff you're pulling is just *not me*. No ma'am, it is *not* in my color scheme. It is *not* me, I'm telling you. And I don't have your skinny hips."

Lady A spit out the pins and tags and interrupted the customer's rant. "Well, baby, maybe sometimes it's just best *not* to always *be* you." All of a sudden, she zipped from the dressing room and flipped onto the empty couch space next to Mitch.

Her sudden appearance surprised him into dropping his notepad. "Is this still a good time?"

"Let me ring her things up. She's done all the damage she's gonna do. She's my last one. I promise."

Mitch settled farther back onto the hollowed-out sofa seat. After he nuzzled for a few seconds, he realized that the two-seater was actually a giant-size sofa-bra. He considered his predicament and slid over to the adjoining cup so that the agitated customer would have a more difficult time seeing him.

After that lady duck-walked past him, loaded down with boxes and bags, Lady A curled up and sat on her knees on the other side. "That last one wore me slap out. I mean it. Hey girls, make sure that Closed sign's lit up. You wanna beer? A little glass a wine? How 'bout a margarita? I think I got the stuff for it."

"No ma'am. I'm good…"

"How will I ever really know that?" She laughed and continued laughing and then stopped on a dime. "Oh, honey, you don't know my humor. That's just who I am." She stopped saying anything and took a deep breath. "Now…talkin' about Lori Leigh and Myron. All of it. It ain't gonna be easy."

"If it makes it any easier, you need to know that I'm just in the exploring stage." He tried to wipe away any pressure or sadness for her. "Maybe it's got some legs to it. The whole thing's always puzzled the hell out a me. And everybody else too, I guess. Can it be a TV show or something for Judge Smack Jack? I just feel like I need to give it a shot. If nothin' else, just understand it a little better."

"This whole town, not just the Cole family, but all of us. When we lost Lori Leigh and Myron, we just let our souls get the root rot. And you know…there ain't no comin' back from the root rot."

"Would you be willing to tell me some things about Lori Leigh or give me names of people I need to talk to who could fill in some puzzle pieces?"

"Oh yeah, I can do ya a list. And if you're askin' about what happened, I've always been torn myself. It seemed to be way too big and horrible to be just some old garden-variety accident. It never did flush, to my way of thinking. I can't quite say it out loud like I want too. Personally, well, maybe I shouldn't say."

"What makes you think it was not an accident?" he asked.

"That's what's got the whole town so tore up. Everybody's always tryin' to come up with that one thing or person to put the blame on. Next thing you know, it's the whole town's playin' the blame game. I can see it sometimes, how havin' a blame is some kind a comfort, I guess. Put an end to it. Start fresh. But not when it comes to Lori Leigh and Myron. Seems like there's a new blame every week."

"What about Sharona Riddle? You think she knows anything?"

"Some people say *she's* one a the blames too, just so you know. I'm sure she'll say just about anything. I already heard she didn't like you comin' to see her. That's a red flag. She'll be at the top a just about anybody's talk-to list. And you best be aware, somebody's bound to bow up on ya, so watch out for who might do that." Lady A dabbed the corner of her eye.

"I've always heard rumors." He said that much, hoping she would take the bait and run with it. "But they're all over the map."

Lady A changed position, stood, and stretched. "Maybe it could be something or somebody nobody's even thought about yet. I think about that sometimes."

"Maybe I ought not to go into all that," Mitch said. "Maybe just go with a side story rather than the whole thing. Main thing's findin' something to make some money on. I'm not just stuck to Myron and Lori Leigh. I'm just tryin' to be straight up with ya."

She sat back on the sofa, but this time on the front edge. "Listen here." She looked around. "It's like I've always heard. Once you start sweepin' the house, you start findin' everything."

There was an awkward broken bridge of silence between them until Lady A cranked up again. Mitch flinched when she spoke.

"Me and Lori Leigh, we had first grade together. Mrs. Jolene Johnson. And that's in the time we went through integration. All that was happening. After that, we were always in the same class. All the way through. Well, you know, up until…" Her eyes filled up fast, as if they were holding back a hundred-year flood. She walked away from him, but she stopped to fluff up a rack of dresses and rearrange some rings and watches. She walked all the way back to the dressing rooms again. Mitch heard two pocket doors slap together.

He didn't want to see Lady A cry. In a short while, he let himself out the front door. Another song cranked up, but he didn't hear enough of it to figure out who it was.

PART III

CHAPTER 21

Over the next two weeks, the dog days of August left the middle part of South Carolina too long on the grill, searing it toward a smoky surrender.

During that stretch, Mitch persuaded the plaintiff and the defendant in the Soothsayer/Mr. Speedo case to sign a contract with *The Judge Smack Jack Show*. As part of the package, the show conditionally offered to pay both parties for an all-expense-paid trip to Hollywood, inclusive of airfare, food, hotel, and even a Beverly Hills Celebrity Home Bus Tour. In exchange, the parties had to agree to sell the rights to their case and then to battle it out in a TV trial. If Judge Smack Jack decided to air the show, then the parties would each receive a $5,000 bonus, and the show would pay whatever monetary verdict the judge awarded, with a cap of $10,000.

To Mitch's amazement, when he drove to Atlanta to present the case, Elkin only had to listen to two minutes of the particulars before he jumped to his feet and declared it as "one of the juiciest set of facts in Smack Jack history." He immediately stroked Mitch a check for $1,500 and sent him on his way to inform the parties they had a done deal and to start with the arrangements.

The next day, Mitch began his trip back to Fountainville to meet with the parties and also with plans to pan for more gold with Kathy Moss at the Fountainville Magistrate's Court. Before he got on the road, he called A.P. but had to leave a message on his answering machine. "Meet me at six o'clock tonight at Sweet Shelby's. I got some news…damn good news…so I'm payin'."

The three-hour trip and a smorgasbord of fuzzy country music stations along Interstate 85 sparked all kinds of giddiness, including ambitious visions of potential stories, maybe even something to impress his old hometown. By the time he crossed the Georgia–South Carolina line somewhere close to Anderson, however, he had decided that he wasn't sure he wanted to troll cases for the rest of his life. But that $1,500 check burning through his wallet continued to invigorate his whole future view. It was a freezing first sip of beer after a long, dry cattle drive.

He swung by Greenville, Simpson Inn, and then finally past the Fountainville city limits. The first thing he spotted after he read the ninety-eight-degree, 3:05 p.m. message on the Judy Woods Insurance sign was Cat Swanger's patrol car partially obscured by a mobile billboard advertising "JAY ROOKS! THE ONE AND ONLY—INTERNATIONALLY ACCLAIMED EVANGELIST AND HYPNOTIST—special guest—October 3rd—Fountainville First Baptist. (Love Offering to Follow the Service)."

He took his foot off the gas, made a right turn, and rolled far enough to get a full view of what Cat Swanger was doing behind that sign. Swanger was laid back in a La-Z Boy, shaded by a beach umbrella. He looked to be hugging a radar gun that had toppled into his lap.

—

He oozed for another half block and parked near Garth's Red Dot Store. Initially he felt a strong wave of civic duty to warn the chief that the clandestine speed-trap cover wasn't working. After he walked a few steps, he thought better of it. Just after he wrangled free from that dilemma, Mitch watched as Bud Culdock's taxi flew past Swanger's hideout and screeched and hunkered to a stop. Culdock then whipped his T-Bird taxi into at least a five-point U-turn, square in the middle of Main Street. Cars coming from both directions stopped at a distance as if anticipating a spectacle. The taxi suddenly skimmied its tires and headed back out of town in a cloudy plume.

The recliner groaned and pitched forward, throwing Swanger as if he were baled hay. The landing smuffed up a dust cloud. He twitched a few times, cockroached onto his back, rocked, rolled, and finally got to his feet. He wasted no time limping toward the middle of the street and bowing up as if he wanted to flush out Wyatt Earp and Doc Holliday.

The drivers in the assembly of bewildered vehicles flung open their doors as far as they would go, squatted, and used them for shields.

Chief Swanger raised both arms, invocation-like, and screamed above the fading wail of Culdock's oppressed taxi engine: "Look at that dayum Culdock...I ought to ticket his ass."

CHAPTER 22

By the time Bud Culdock pulled up to his double-wide a few minutes later, the late-afternoon summer heat was conjuring up gusts mean enough to tip his taxi. He began to sweat, and his hands ached. His heartbeat had jumped into a full gallop when he spotted Swanger's partially hidden car, but after he cleared the town, it gradually slowed to a trot.

When the fat raindrops splatted the windshield all at once and the wind punched his car from side to side, he couldn't see anything but the cascade across the glass and the distant trees that seemed to be trying to erase his picture. He stared through the glass, and he returned to a recurring childhood memory.

—

It was his birthday party, his fifth. His parents gifted him with a toy parachute man. He would wrap the yellow parachute around the toy soldier, fling it, and then marvel as it circled, swung, and rode into the grass. For hours he threw the parachute man…until it was almost dusk. His mother called out the back door for supper, but he couldn't resist one more throw. He wrapped the parachute just like always and gave it his very best heave. It was the most beautiful flight of the day, and the parachute man sailed against the fiery sunset. Out of nowhere, a rush of wind inflated the chute and carried his prize beyond the grass and the house and into a giant oak. It sank high up and deep into thick leaves. He ran to the tree, helplessly looking up. He wrapped his arms around the trunk as if he might be able to shake it free, and he watched as the parachute strings looped and tangled with each gust until his prize toy was more a part of the tree than a parachute man.

—

After a few more minutes, the storm subsided, and all was calm. The shoe-shop taxi man stepped out and removed the wet Chicago Cabs magnets from the doors and dropped them onto the floorboard carpet mat, hoping they'd be dry by morning.

CHAPTER 23

"Oh, Sweetie, Sweetie," Sharona Riddle hissed like a punctured inner tube. "We lived us up another day. Even though we got Mr. Judas with his bag a silver. Makin it *all* bubble up again. He's out there somewhere. Can't you feel it?"

"Miss Sharona, don't tell me you wakin' up with all ya guns blazin'," Sweetie said.

"Let's just keep on growing on our vine." Miss Sharona revved up again. "Like we one a Mr. Hendershot's muscadines. And somehow…somehow, someway, we got to get a hold a that fruity sweetness on the inside. But mostly, we got to get that thick skin. Muscadine skin. It'll be like the God a Jacob bein' our fortress."

CHAPTER 24

About an hour after Mitch witnessed the Main Street ruckus between Culdock and Swanger, the embarrassed sun dipped for cover behind a stand of longleaf pines, stoic and impenetrable. Since he had a half hour to kill before dinner at Sweet Shelby's, he took a seat on a bench in front of Jeter Garrett's Barber Shop. He had gotten his first real haircut there. A flattop. His mama let him choose it from a wall chart featuring COOL AND POPULAR HAIR STYLES FOR COOL MEN.

The shop looked closed, and a motor whirred underneath the hypnotic barber pole. After a few minutes, he stepped over and peeked inside and saw that Jeter still had the two wall-length mirrors. The way they faced each other made an infinite tunnel of diminishing reflections. During haircuts, he could never take his eyes from them for very long, and Jeter even warned him once not to look too far into the tunnel. "You'll see ya whole future and ruin all ya surprises."

Before he walked away, he spotted a faded wall space where the hairstyle chart had been. And there below, the comb vending machine was still in its regular place like a referee in a boxing match between the past and what was to come. He instantly thought of Myron and his beloved clip-comb that he fastened to his shirt pocket. Myron never wasted an opportunity to doctor the two red cowlicks in the front. During rounds of golf, he routinely pulled the comb out before tee shots and even sometimes before lining up longer putts.

Two blocks ahead he could see the roof-mounted Sweet Shelby's Café sign. It flashed and cast yellow-green light on the sidewalk as he stepped along. Behind and within the letters, sphinx moths and big dipper fireflies air danced while stag beetles and Baltimore snouts buzzed against the pulsating letters.

Just inside the door at Sweet Shelby's, there loomed the infamous Chef's Weather Vane. It looked to be a combination beehive box and hat rack highlighted by a bronze chanticleer on top. The weather vane had proven to be a popular photograph spot for visitors, and the café owner, Shelby Jean Shillinglaw, took full credit for the strategic decision to position it there as the café's centerpiece. That required her to relocate the hostess station even though it awkwardly impeded larger patrons from squeezing through to the dining area.

Fierce winds had sheared it off the top of the town hall cupola during the nontornadoes of '73. Nobody could swear to its provenance from that point, but Chef Juicy Drake somehow got his hands on it and came up with the idea to use its directional boards to chalk in the nightly specials. The locals knew that the NORTH and SOUTH boards were also code signals to warn them of the current mood of its quicksilver owner.

Mitch read the special as HAMBURGER STEAK-N-ONIONS CHEESE POTATO/HOUSE SALAD. He couldn't remember if NORTH was good or bad. He was going back and forth about it when the kitchen door flew open, and there was Sweet Shelby herself, with her stack of red hair brushing against the top of the door frame. "Well, look here now… what in the worrell…you've got to be kiddin' me." She rushed Mitch's table and pulled him right into her chest before he could climb to his feet. "Hey there, angel love…and Billy's best all-time buddy. I could just eat you up with a spoon." Mitch couldn't sit or stand and just levitated there until she let him loose and slid into the other booth all in one seamless move.

"Miss Shelby…you're a pearl in a mean ol' world," Mitch said. "And you got it smellin' like heaven on earth in here. I'm waitin' on A.P."

"That A.P. Thackston…he's always been soooo good to me and mine. Specially bein' so patient with me and Billy," she said and somehow dabbed each eye corner with her pinky fingers in spite of her long nails. "He tried with Billy. He really did. And here you are, right out a Billy's good times. You want a sweet tea? Hold on."

Before he could get a word in, she was already disappearing into the kitchen door. It swung and wonked about four times until she hip-bumped it again on the way out, balancing three teas on a try.

"Thank you, ma'am. But it's just me and A.P."

"Two a these are for A.P. He likes two teas all at once," she said. "One for knockin' out thirst. And then the other's just for taste. That's accordin' to him." She lined up the teas. "Now, I'll do two for you too, if you want it that way." Mitch waved off her offer and took a sip. When he looked up again, he noticed a framed picture of Myron and Billy just over Miss Shelby's shoulder. They were both holding golf trophies. "Nice picture there."

She turned and smiled. "Oh, you lookin' at my Wall a Fame." She jumped out and walked to the other end of the room and pointed to another, smaller black-and-white. "You made it too."

Mitch squinted and saw what looked like a baseball team photo. "Weren't y'all on Tex-ize together?" she asked, and then stepped back from it. "Billy used to tell me all kinds a stories about that team."

"Yes, we were. Now that's something," Mitch said to himself.

Shelby returned and sat again. Suddenly one of the waitresses jabbed the kitchen door holding a folded piece of paper.

"Excuse me, y'all…I hate to interrupt…Miss Shelby, Chef Juicy said to get this right out."

Shelby snatched the note and held it at arm's length as if it had the flames of burning Rome on it. "I ain't got time for foolishness…tell Juicy to get that man on the phone…and just say this one thing: get me those laminated menus, or get me the name a somebody who *will*."

Mitch wondered again if he had walked in and read the wrong weather vane board. As soon as the waitress scooted off into the shadows, A.P. in perfect timing, appeared at the booth. He bent and pecked Miss Shelby on the cheek. "Look at my sweet teas all lined up nice and neat," he said and sat close to Miss Shelby.

Mitch watched her press both palms on her cheeks and close her eyes. And then she transformed into a verbal fireworks show, detonating subject after subject. First, questions for Mitch—what his love life looked like, and what a troller was, and what he was doing talking to Sharona Riddle, Lady A, and even Kathy Moss. And then she circled back to asking what it was like working for Judge Smack Jack, and, every now and then, she tied in a Billy story. Mitch managed to squeeze in portions of responses to her questions, but the Sweet Shelby Express usually rammed right down the track without stopping for passengers.

In the middle of the whole reunion spectacle, a waitress entered and accepted their orders for two specials. Then the next round of fireworks ensued, this time a little more about Billy—how hard it was to raise him after his parents died, what it was that really changed about him after Lori Leigh and Myron died, how he had lived the last years in a small shed on Ricky Hammond's property, and how she hadn't had the strength to go through it to clean it out. She made a passing reference to the two-headed dog, which Mitch was understanding to be a story known to everyone except him. The last big flurry included her advice on how Mitch might be able to get the story of Lori Leigh and Myron on TV or maybe even a movie. "It would make a fiiine love story. Sure would," she repeated several times. "A.P. clued me in a little bit."

The waitress swooped in with the two specials and a platter full of biscuits without a sound. "Oh, I can't wait," Mitch said.

Before either Mitch or A.P. could cut their first bite, Miss Shelby's arms became railroad crossing bars. "A.P., why don't you bless it." After A.P. struggled through the blessing, she stepped away.

Before either man had taken his second bite, she was back.

"Oh, honey, how'd you and Miss Sharona getcha wires so crossed?" she asked and poured tea refills. "The whole town's talkin' about Mitch Beam doin' this and doin' that. Tryin' to figure if you're friend or foe."

"I thought my Pink House meeting was gonna be kind of a nice warm-up," he said. "But that nurse a hers, Sweetie something. We was oil and water…"

"If y'all need to talk some more, I can pay a visit. I can be a peacemaker when I need to. We're lifetime friends, you know." Shelby picked at the cheese on top of A.P.'s potato. "Me and Sharona's been tight since we were little. Before integration. I been meanin' to pay her a visit anyway. Think on it."

"Miss Sharona's still the main one for you; that's what I say," A.P. said quickly on the heels of Shelby's offer. "She's done picked her lot in Beulah Land. You know what I'm sayin'. And let me say what I always say about time: It don't spin its tires in the mud. Nope."

After Shelby stepped away to greet some of the other tables, Mitch and A.P. ate in silence. Then Mitch remembered the main thing he wanted to do. He pulled out six fifty-dollar bills. He laid them softly on the table and pushed them toward A.P. "Sold my story, boss...the one I told you about." Mitch smiled. "Here's some payback. Lettin' me stay. Eatin' all ya food."

"You don't owe me one penny," A.P. said, pushing the money back. "I didn't expect—"

"Nope. You saved my ass. Let me do this." Mitch picked up the cash, folded it, and wedged it between A.P.'s fingers. "Since I'm on a roll, I got to find me another story, hopefully up this way. You okay if I—"

"You know you don't have to ask," A.P. said. He smoothed out the stack of fifties and placed them lengthwise in his wallet. "You welcome at Thackston Manor anytime."

"I need me another story," Mitch said. "I'll see what Shelby might can work out with Miss Sharona. I got Kathy Moss helpin' me too." Mitch finished his hamburger steak and took one last sip of tea. When he and A.P. exited past the weather vane, the EAST-WEST boards had already been wiped clean. "Now, A.P., what's all this I keep hearin' about some two-headed dog?"

CHAPTER 25

After dinner at Sweet Shelby's, Mitch drove back in a light mist to A.P.'s farmhouse. There was a lot of thunder, but no wind or heavy rain ever followed. Along the way he saw that there was a pretty big crowd at the Scuffletown Dance Barn. He slowed to see if he could make out the ruins of the Stairley Mansion, but the parking lot lights surrounding the dance barn obscured everything about the surrounding landscape.

A few minutes later, his headlights swept across A.P.'s front porch, and A.P. was sitting on a rocker caressing a big bottle of something. Moths and gnats showed off in the sudden spray of light.

Mitch climbed the steps and got a closer view of what A.P. was holding. Mitch grabbed the neck of the Jack Daniel's bottle and poured himself a good two fingers' worth. He grunted when he only landed part of his rear in the other rocker, but he didn't spill a drop. "You see that?" he asked A.P.

"I saw you just about wasted some good whiskey," A.P. said.

"I miss it up here," Mitch said. "Smells like honeysuckle, and throw in that cool breeze." He took a sip that burned a trail from his lips to the back of his throat. That made him forget about the cooler air.

"What's Columbia like?" A.P. asked. He reached and poured Mitch another sip.

"Down there, at night, it's just sticky. Like what I'm picturin' hell must be like. And it stays like that all the way to mid-November. The only time we get a decent breeze is when a thunderstorm's on top a your ass," Mitch said and took a smaller sip.

A.P. broke the silence and started to rock. "That was some kind a good eatin' tonight. And thanks for catchin' the tab."

Mitch felt like he needed to say something. He pushed to get a gentle rock going. He took a sip that mostly touched his lips, and they quickly went numb again. "If it was up to me, I'd give Shelby Shillinglaw the Nobel Peace Prize."

"Why not?" A.P. said. "She's a saint. Poor gal's takin' Billy's death real hard. You do know she took Billy in when it was just a matter of time?" A.P. said. "And then he passed."

"She was his aunt, right?" Mitch said.

"You're right. Billy's her nephew. I mean 'was.' No other kin. She did all she could," A.P. said. "She did all she could. That's the way I saw it."

"Well…" Mitch didn't quite know how to ask it. "When you gonna tell me the story about that two-headed dog?" he asked with a shaky voice. "People look at me like I'm crazy when I ask about it."

As the cricket skeeps faded, Mitch's engine was popping gum as it cooled down. "Yeah, Billy. He was a damn mess," A.P. said. "And if you want the full story, pour yourself a right sizable snort, and then sit back for a ride. It all starts with Billy," A.P. said and then took another shot himself.

"Oh yeah. Gimme the whole spiel," Mitch said.

"You got to be the only one who ain't heard it. You ain't pullin' my leg, are ya? Well, here goes. We had us a Randy Willis house goin' up. And he builds the big-uns. We had just roughed in the plumbing. And you know how it goes. We were waitin' for the county to come inspect before anything else could be done.

"I had both Ricky Hammond and Billy helpin' me back then. Just so happens, I had to go into Greenville to get some pipes for a sewer fall line. Since there was a lull, it seemed like a good time for it." A.P. stopped and wiped his forehead. "So against my better judgment, I left them two knuckleheads behind."

"When was this?" Mitch asked. He dragged his rocker a little closer so that he could hear A.P. over another rumble of thunder and the gentle smacking of tulip poplar branches against the house.

"Oh, 'bout two years after you left for college. Does that make it four years after Lori Leigh and Myron? That's about right, I'd say. Yeah, our college boy left us in the dust." A.P. took another whiskey shot. "Ricky and Billy always got the work done okay. *Always*, believe it or not. It just took 'em longer, with all them smoke breaks. That's what they called 'em." A.P. stopped rocking for a few seconds.

"So, what were they doin'?" Mitch asked to get the story train back on the track again. He had an idea about the answer, but he wanted to make sure A.P. had it right.

"Gettin' high, mostly. And not the usual liquor or beer high. Not even marijuana. It was things like sniffin' paint, gas fumes, even pipe dope… you know, that goo you rub on pipe threads. And spray paint too. Billy had this thing for spray paint." A.P. stood abruptly to brush a couple of no-see-ums out of his hair. "I think it was Sharona Riddle told some of us how to handle a situation where the no-see-ums are gettin' down in ya hair. She said, 'It ain't nothin' but a man brushin' up against the Tree a Knowledge, and you best be getting knees to the floor.'"

A.P. sank back into his rocker. "Hell, you might not believe this. A couple a times I caught 'em snortin' good ol'-fashioned Coca-Colas. Whoever thought a doin' that?" A.P. asked.

"What the hell?" Mitch said.

"And they both did *fine* plumb work for me. That's why I kept 'em on," A.P. said. Then he stepped to the other side of the porch. He pulled out a tobacco pouch from his back pocket. Mitch studied the way A.P. struggled to open it up. He finally pinched off enough for a chew, and he tucked it deep into the side of his mouth under his gumline. He poked at it a couple of times.

Mitch thought about how A.P. made chewing tobacco look like it might be worth a try.

"So," A.P. said, warming up again, "I got back from town with the pipes, and Ricky and Billy were flat out gone. I waited, but then I went ahead and crawled up under the house." A.P. cleared his throat.

"You tellin' me they sniffed Coca-Colas up their nose?" Mitch asked. "That don't seem right, wastin' good Cocolas like that."

"I heard it gives some kind a buzz. And that's all that mattered to them two," A.P. said. "Anyway, I remember it was a low-ass crawl space. I definitely remember that. I was in there about fifty feet, sixty feet maybe, and damn if it didn't hit me. I done left my plumb in the truck. Down in the console. So, with none a my damn helpers around, I commenced to backin' out, ass-first all the way back." A.P. spit a stream off the side of the porch. "So out a nowhere, while half my ass was hangin' out a that crawl space hatch, I heard a horrible commotion like a rockslide. And it really would a been better if it had a been a rockslide. So here comes Ricky and Billy, my two slack-ass helpers. Breathin' hard, eyes flarin'. Snot comin' out both their noses, and Ricky kept sayin' for me to come see somethin'…and then he said forget that, and I better go get the law.

"I got myself out that hatch door, and I tried askin' them to calm down and tell me what the hell it was, but they had the shakes so bad, and they was coughin' and runnin' around in circles. I grabbed the first thing I saw, which was a broken-off shovel. And then that's when Billy started sayin' it was 'a dog with two heads.' And then, ten seconds later, he started sayin' it was 'a *giant* dog with two heads.' And that's when I remember thinkin' I might should a grabbed me something a little bigger than that stubby shovel.

"They walked me farther up to a stand of weeds and scrub oak, and just when more animal growlin' came out, I stuck that shovel into them weeds like this. I then made me a gap so I could see, and there it was all right. Bigger 'n hell. And you know what? It *did* have two heads all right… sure as hell did. *But*—that was because it *was two dogs*. Two damn dogs gettin' it on. And so I poked at 'em a couple a times till they pulled apart, and away they went, squawkin' the whole way." A.P. took a big breath and laughed a little. "I should a known better."

"What did they do after that?" Mitch asked.

"Nothing," A.P. said quickly. "And then when I explained about it bein' two dogs and what was goin' on, they just stared at me like I'd just told one a the biggest fish whoppers of all time. Pissed me off good. Two-headed dog…Really? Ain't that some shit?"

Off in the dark, unseen distance, a freight train chicka-chicked through the middle of Fountainville and into neighboring Simpson Inn. The cross-arm bell at the Scuffletown–Main Street crossing clankled, and both A.P. and Mitch stared at the ground boards of the front porch until the ringing stopped. They sipped their whiskey in silence.

A.P. cleared his throat a couple of times, and then he began to bounce the toes of his right foot. Mitch knew those were A.P.'s signals that he had something else to say. He waited.

"You know, we ain't ever getting over it. When it's somebody young that passes, especially somebody like Lori Leigh and Myron, it won't leave ya alone. And when it happens in a small town, it ain't like havin' all ya tires go flat. It's more like havin' ya whole car stolen, and then on top a that, it's like somebody comes walkin' up and says, 'We're sorry, but you're not even allowed to walk if you wanna go somewhere. So you wake up every morning knowin' you gotta crawl anywhere you wanna go. And then it feels even a thousand times worse'n that, if you wanna know the truth."

CHAPTER 26

March 31, 1978

On the Friday after Easter, on the lawn in front of Fonda's Muffler Shop, an early-morning shower had knocked down petals from pink-and-white dogwoods and fanned them out in perfect circles. Most of the out-of-town reporters assumed that the petals were intentionally strewn affectations, and they couldn't be talked out of writing up their stories that way.

Jimmy Fonda's plans, three months in the making, were to send formal invitations to newspapers, magazines, and radio and television stations all around the country in order to lure them to Fountainville for the unveiling of a statue to honor what the invitation described as "the Father of Clean Air and Sound."

His muffler shop had fallen on lean times due to some unfortunate publicity, and the business decline placed Fonda on the brink of going out of business.

The ceremony traffic began streaming into town just after the early rain. Everything was set to start at noon, and around ten, the traffic became steady and jammed up cars on Main Street all the way west into the neighboring town limits of Simpson Inn and all the way east close to the edge of Edwards Crossroads. Many frustrated drivers gave up hope, parked on the shoulder, and formed an exodus into town.

Weeks earlier, Jimmy gave Chief Swanger a heads-up on the scope of the invitation and the potential for traffic congestion, but the chief didn't take it seriously. Not until midmorning, when all the calls came pouring in to the station. He scrambled to deputize a handful of trustee prisoners to flip their vests around from orange to yellow so they could serve as traffic directors. He persuaded them to help out by promising commutations of their community trash pickup sentences, which, he learned after the fact, he technically didn't have any legal authority to order.

A horde of reporters, photographers, and videographers swarmed around a large object that was completely obscured by two white sheets. The sheets appeared to be duct-taped together at all corners. The visitors snapped pictures and shot video of Jimmy Fonda's shop building as well as his refurbished sign. The veiled object appeared to stand about six to seven feet tall, and there was speculation about the material used for the statue and whether there was a proper pedestal. Someone declared that any legitimate statue should always consist of marble or bronze and not one of the lesser metals. Most of the scuttlebutt, however, swirled around guessing the identity of the Father of Clean Air and Sound. Some suggested the likelihood of someone like Ralph Nader, John Muir, Rachel Carson, or maybe even President Teddy Roosevelt. Some other rumor started that Fonda had been childhood friends with Fortson Brent, a local musician who had made it big as a recording star. Brent had infamously stormed the stage at the finals of the Miss South Carolina Pageant two years earlier to promote the cleanup of the polluted Reedy River. "Just put two and two together," one voice belted out. Most went along with the possibility the statue would be Fountainville Councilwoman, former Miss Fountainville, and Second Runner-Up Miss South Carolina Judy Woods. She later founded and organized the Annual Fountainville Cleanup Day. A small betting pool at Betty Jane's Diner established Miss Woods as the odds-on favorite.

At five minutes till twelve, Jimmy Fonda emerged from the front door of his shop. The smack of the storm door temporarily quieted the crowd. He was wearing a denim suit with a Texas tie and boots, and his hair bun was tucked under a tan fedora. He solemnly strode across the lawn, past his sign and the phalanx of reporters and cameras. Flashbulbs popped and smoked all around him. His skeptical fellow Fountainvillians, who had segregated themselves from the media and the out-of-towners, slowly got caught up in the moment and the bright national spotlight hoopla, and they were the ones who instigated pockets of clapping that grew into a pretty hardy ovation.

When he arrived at the statue, he pulled an index card from inside his jean jacket and waited for the crowd to get quiet. He cleared his throat a couple of times and began to speak.

"My fellow citizens of the towns of Fountainville, Simpson Inn, Mulkey, Edwards Crossroads, Peppletown, Rhine Shoals, Turner Junction, Quillen Mills, and Ben Davis Court, and also all the reporters who accepted the invitation to attend this ceremony, some of whom came from all around the states of South Carolina, Georgia, North Carolina, and even as far as New York City...the *New York Times*, y'all..."

"Aw, get the hell on with it, Fonda...we got lunch to eat," somebody hollered and set off a crackle of clapping and laughter.

"I hear ya," Jimmy said and cleared his throat again. "I have searched the history of Fountainville and all the towns I just named that make up what we call the Golden Crescent, and I did all I could to research the entire state of South Carolina. I even called up University of South Carolina Professor and noted historian Walter Edgar, and to our best knowledge, this very statue here is unique for being the very first of its kind and purpose. That is, it's the only known statue to honor and celebrate cleaning the air to make it devoid of noxious gas and also of sound pollution, which, I might add, is what Fonda Mufflers strives to do. So without further delay, I give you the one and only..." Jimmy Fonda stopped and yanked one of the ropes, which successfully pulled away one of the sheets, but the duct tape held the other sheet so firmly that several in the crowd had to grab the other part and tug it to the ground. "I give you..." he began again, "the Monument to Mighty Co."

Some in the crowd gasped. Others moved in closer for a better look and to read the bronze plaque at the statue figure's feet. After a few seconds, there was an amalgamation of laughter, and murmuring, and what the reporters later described in their newspaper stories as "a pocket of silent indignation" and "startled consternation and contemplation," and an "awkward eternity of time when there was confusion over whether to laugh or cheer."

The plaque read:

Monument to Mighty Co
Honoring the Muffler Men of the World,
And the Art of Removing Repugnant Gas and Sound.

Jimmy Fonda
Proprietor and Operator of Fonda's Muffler Shop.
"We're Fonda your business."

Fonda walked right up to the statue and wrapped an arm around what was apparently a man-shaped figure. "Picasso-like," one reporter said. And Fonda told one reporter it was made completely of the parts from a car's exhaust system. Some contemplated out loud that one upraised part seemed to be sending a signal of some significance. After a few seconds, while Jimmy continued to hold on, the reporters and cameramen gathered around him in a cloud of flashing witnesses.

One reporter was heard to ask, "Mister Fonda, why? Why a...what is it? Why a muffler man and not a real person?"

Fonda chuckled, and then his face twisted into a shape no one had ever seen on Jimmy Fonda before. "Well, let's just say he's a friend a mine. And one that's worth keeping." After answering that question, he turned away and walked a faster pace back into his muffler shop.

———

In the weeks and months that followed the unveiling of Mighty Co, the story became a national sensation in newspapers, magazines, and even some national news broadcasts. The photograph of Fonda hugging his muffler man even appeared in *Timeless Magazine*. As a result people from all over the country made their way to Fountainville to see the muffler man and to have their picture made with him. The local merchants reaped immeasurable commerce and soon talked Jimmy up as a town leader and celebrity.

Soon, without explanation, the gossip about Jimmy Fonda and the rumored faulty work on Myron Parsons's GTO exhaust system disappeared, and customers brought their business back and saved Fonda. Many folks gave credit to Jimmy's good timing and good marketing strategy. Fonda, though, knew there was evidence that his beloved statue had a lot to do with it.

PART IV

CHAPTER 27

The next morning the sun burst across the glass doors at the front of the magistrate's court. Mitch stopped there for a few seconds to admire how the backdrop of moving traffic spurled the colors in the condensation.

He pushed in, and a cowbell clonked his entrance. The fluorescent lights zwoomed and cast a sallow tone as if the office was still struggling to wake up. He knew to look for Clerk Moss in the security nests near the corners, but he saw and heard nothing.

"Is that my Smack Jack man?" Mitch was pretty sure that was her voice that crackled from the ceiling speakers. He realized for the first time how much she sounded like Lady A, and he smiled. "Be right with ya."

He lingered near the front counter. Coffee poppled from the break room. He flipped through a display of Wanted posters and snickered at the one emblazoned with Chief Cat Swanger's photo. Just below was a request for information on some suspicious fires near the Scuffletown Dance Barn. Clerk Moss sneaked up on him while he was deep reading about the fires.

"I got another one for ya, Mitch Beam. Step yourself through that swinging door. Let me show off my fancy new file room. We added that since your last time."

"You're the doll of 'em all, Miss Kathy."

She took off, and he did his best to keep up with her as the short train zipped through a maze of file cabinets made up of various sizes and styles, but almost all of them in warm shades of tan and army green. "This one right here," she blurted and braked into a slight skid. She reached into a desk and pulled out a single key rubbed raw around the edges. She swiveled to unlock a smaller file box covered by a shoe buffing cloth. "See if ya Smack Jack man'll like this one. It's really all about a race horse. A horse named *Magnificent Malochi*. You'll see what I mean once you get into it. Good old-timey mix a horse-tradin' and bruised egos." When she finished and presented the manila folder to him, almost simultaneously a whole bank of fluorescent lights clicked and instantly bathed them both in new light.

Magnificent Malochi was foaled and trained in the hamlet of Green Pond, South Carolina, and he went on to win the Jim Dandy Stakes, the Gulfstream Handicap, and several high-stakes races along the East Coast and at Keeneland in Kentucky. His famous sire, Force of Nomenclature, won the Preakness and the Belmont Stakes after not being invited to race in the Kentucky Derby. The owner of *Magnificent Malochi* was Snood Trotter, a South Carolina legend internationally acclaimed in the sport of thoroughbred racing. Trotter once described his successful racehorse as "just as unpredictable and entertaining as his namesake." He was referring to R&B music legend Eskew Reeder, who usually performed under the stage name the *Magnificent Malochi*. Trotter was never totally forthcoming on how he had discovered the horse, and in an interview with the Greenville News, he would only say that his horse was "the truest diamond in the rough there ever was." Snood Trotter later sold his successful race horse to Gilreath Farms, and *Magnificent Malochi* retired to stud there. He went on to sire several successful horses, including Eat Buzzy's Dust, Make Em Talk, and Can't Make Me Drink, all three of which won a number of races and substantial winnings for their owners.

Mitch studied Clerk Moss as she scuttled back to lock the secret file drawer. The way she threw her hands out and spun around, it looked to him almost like she was praising heaven for something. "These my copies, Miss Kathy?" he asked as he made a move for his wallet.

"Oh yeah, honey," she answered immediately. "You get all these copies on the house. 'Cause let me tell you flat out. If you can get these parties signed up for your show and off my docket, you'll be doin' the wheels a justice a *huge* favor. Yep, no charge for copies. I'm just thankin' you in advance."

He looked at the caption on the complaint and read the allegations of the first few paragraphs. "Miss Moss, you won't believe this, but I know at least a little bit about both sides in this case. Might give me an edge when I try to sign 'em up. This one's got some po-tential." Mitch rolled up his copy of the complaint and started to drum it against the side of his head and then along the edge tops of several file cabinets.

When he made his way to the front, he drummed it some more against the counter with increased ferocity.

"Don't handle it like that," she cawed and snatched it out of his hand. She rolled the pages back the opposite way and pressed them against the countertop with the bottom of her forearm. Mitch saw her jaw jut out like she wanted to get even for something. "Mitch Beam." She used the sides of her hands to squeegee the rills of sweat from her cheeks. "See here...all a my case files in here...every single one. They're all full a half lies and half truths. But in this world, those are the hooks that justice hangs on. Now... show at least a little reverence and see if you can work something to the good out a what I'm giving you. Act like you somebody."

Mitch picked up the complaint and the file folder again and pressed them softly to his chest so as not to create any more wrinkles. "Thank you, Miss Kathy. You're an iron hand in a velvet glove." When he pulled the door, it tripped the cowbell again and snagged on the door mat as it closed. He instantly breathed in the wind from an approaching thunderstorm.

Over a row of Main Street storefronts where Sweet Shelby's, Culdock's Sole Music, and Garrett's Barber Shop rubbed their brick shoulders, the grayer angles of the downpour started to hiss over the rooftops. He thought about the need to protect his new case and took off running for his parked car. He unleashed a leg-flying jaunt that looked more like a bush-hog dragging a limb. He made it inside before the really fat drops splatted the windshield, and while he waited, he thought a little more about the parties in the new lawsuit.

He cringed thinking about the plaintiff, Berry Gilreath, who was the Ivy League–educated owner and CEO of Gilreath Farms. He remembered him from high school as an obnoxious know-it-all. Mitch never mixed with him. He was, by all accounts, "big boned" and so massively tall he had to stoop to pass through most door frames. His lasting legacy was that he never played any sports, which pissed off all the coaches and bamboozled pretty much the whole town.

The defendant in the suit, Samp Reames, was a part-time evangelist and the owner of the Bless Your Heart Pawn Shop. Mitch knew that if Reames wasn't on a revival circuit somewhere, he would be pretty easy to find.

Mitch had no doubt that Berry Gilreath would be the tougher one to persuade to sign up for the show. He was just as uneasy knowing he'd have to cross the lower edge of the Gilreath Farm land to get to Berry Gilreath's gated driveway. It would be steep and rutted out with slick mud and possibly too difficult for his Cutlass to climb.

After the rain eased up, he sat in the quiet for a few minutes hearing only an occasional spillet of rain that the wind blew down from leaf tips and overhead wires. Bee and butterfly wings and guts held firmly to each wiper blade. Several times he gripped the steering wheel only to let go. He knew he'd have to drive right through the spot where Bud Culdock had found Myron and Lori Leigh. He turned the key and spun out briefly on the wet pavement, leaving a trail of exhaust that mortared the gaps between the parked cars and, after a few seconds, completely dissipated.

CHAPTER 28

After retrieving the new file from Miss Moss, Mitch got the strongest urge to keep pressing forward to the Gilreath Farm. "Maybe this rush'll help me ram right through it," he thought.

He cleared the congested Five Points intersection and gathered speed going down Scuffletown's biggest hill. At the last second, he dodged a possum sprawled out exactly where his left tires would have wreaked more road-kill carnage. He wondered if the creature was still alive or just following its natural instinct for confronting an approaching danger. After he successfully straddled it, he continued to check his rearview mirror until the possum was almost out of sight. He considered turning around to see if it had wandered off, but he was under a stronger spell to keep going.

He passed over another crest and rounded a curved section overarched by the lush entanglements of sweet gum, white oak, and holly. As the road opened up again, there was a giant black plume of smoke gushing upward beyond the distant tree line. It looked to be about a mile away, and the top of its column mixed gray into the swirling ground clouds. "Dark smoke. Most likely a structure," he thought.

When the grassy slopes of the Gilreath Farm came into view, the lights from a pair of firetrucks, a circle of ambulances, and what looked to be a police vehicle—"That's Cat Swanger right there," he mumbled—bounced off the low clouds and rolled out in circles to make a disco floor of the entire valley all the way up to the burning dance barn.

He briefly recalled the Cat Swanger arson poster back at the court-house. As he closed in behind a small line of vehicles slowing to a stop, he was close enough to make out a T-shaped object protruding from the peak of the dance barn's partially collapsed roof line. The smoke was growing thicker and darker and rolling in waves into the trees. The streams of water looping from the fire hoses hit the flames and caused larger billows that wrestled the edges of the blaze.

The firetrucks freight-trained across Scuffletown to stop traffic. When Mitch saw the scope of the calamity, he pulled over and cut off the engine, amazed by another Scuffletown spectacle. The flames began moving faster and soon engulfed most of the dance barn section. When the roadside wall collapsed, the T-shaped object looked more like the tail end of a small airplane. When the flames shifted, the smoke whipped outward to make it impossible for him to see any more details. Around one corner of the dance barn, where the bingo tables were usually set, people spurted from the doors like blood from a head wound. They shouted, waved arms, and ran about in broken circles. Several carried or dragged all kinds of items and cast them into piles that slowly took on the shapes of Picasso figures.

Mitch was acutely mesmerized by several cotton-dressed women who appeared to be covering the junk piles by throwing quilts and blankets, some with blue, red, and white ribbons hanging from the edges. When one petite woman accidentally got plunked and swallowed up by an awkward quilt toss, Mitch jumped out and began a slow trot toward her. As he descended the hill, he tried his best to avoid slipping in the mud and wet grass. He watched with relief as the buried woman flailed, squirmed, and eventually emerged from under the cover. She pushed up to her knees and climbed to her feet. She wiggled her top, which had become twisted over her head, exposing one of her breasts outside her bra. Once she had taken case of that business, she took off for the woman who had misfired the quilt. They came together and appeared to exchange words, and the smaller woman stretched her arm high, as if she wanted to pull off a branch from the closest oak. She locked herself in that position for a few seconds, pushed up on her tiptoes, and whomped the taller woman twice across the neck and chest. Seconds after the blows, the lady covered her breasts and squalled, loud enough to be heard all the way back into town, "My new boobs! My girls!" The smaller one then sprang toward the other cotton-dressed lady, who was in full gawk, and she pancaked her deeply into the wet grass. They wiggled for a while like upended turtles, putting on a show for the firemen and first responders, who watched with a two-alarm structure blaze as a backdrop.

Mitch saw one of the firemen drop his grip on a hose, pull the combatants apart, and shove them in two different directions. He ran back to resume extinguishing the fire.

Mitch slowed his descent into a copperhead stillness and then attempted to blend into the field of wet fescue and tufts of taller ryegrass. He felt the saturated ground finding its way into his cracked soles. The hiss-pop of flames and wood mixed with the hoots and hollers of those who were struggling to put out the fire.

He watched the aggressive smaller woman give one more shove to the wounded boob-job lady, and then she chased after the other lady for a few steps until that lady tripped and fell into muddy hardpan. She turned away from her two vanquished foes and gracefully wrapped some sort of cape around her shoulders. After a few paces, she stopped to remove her sandals, which were caked with mud and weeds. To Mitch's disappointment, she began walking barefoot up the slope and directly toward where he had dug his heels into the hillside. When she had gotten to within about fifty feet, he recognized that the smaller lady was Amelia Stone. Lady A herself. "Those two huzzies…" she hollered. "You know they both blamed me for all a that down there."

"Well, you certainly took care a that." Which was all he could come up with. "I was on my way down there when the quilt got you."

"You know…neither one a those rednecks had the courtesy to say 'I'm sorry' or nothin'." Lady A stopped walking and pulled her hair into a bun. "I'm a mess. Don't look."

"Oh, you look fine…and that right hook…hoooweee." Mitch put his hand over his mouth so she wouldn't see him smiling.

"I can't believe they said it was *all* because a me." She put her hands on her hips. "And both of 'em are longtime customers too. Rednecks…"

"How's a plane crash your fault?"

"Well…" She stopped in midsentence. "It was pulling my banner. I guess that's how. I do admit that. Whenever it's Season-Pleazin time, he flies my banner. You remember Rocky Steading, I know. He's been back from Vietnam for a few years. Anyway, he says he's a professional pilot. Flies crop dusters and banners too. And you see what happens when I try to help somebody? He flies planes for some a these rock and roll bands. Makes good money, I hear."

"I saw the smoke way back there. Rocky ain't dead, is he?" he asked, hoping that he understood correctly.

"You can't kill a *real* fool. At least not in no regular way," she said.

"Lucky as hell. Damn lucky," Mitch said and twisted back toward the barn when he heard another wall collapse. "Anybody in there?"

"No, thank goodness. Just some old quilts that won some fair ribbons. That's what those two whacked-out quilt flingers got so worked up about. I think I set 'em straight, though."

"He's got to be banged up," Mitch said and waited for some gory details.

"Oh…somehow, he claimed he timed his jump just right. And right before impact. And he claims he landed in a stack a baled hay." Lady A laughed and clapped her hands. "I guess I should be glad he ain't dead."

"That's some a the best damn luck I ever heard of," he said.

"That's nothing short of the Lord. He was lookin' out for me, no doubt, Mitch Beam."

He saw that look on her face again, like she might just rare back and coldcock him too if he didn't choose the right words.

"I went and found him, and just as soon as I got within earshot, he started whinin' about his back. And I told him, 'You look here. You can just flat out get over a hurt back, 'cause there's a fire headin' right for your butt. And then I told him I wasn't payin' a dime for all the bad publicity."

"What caused it?" Mitch wanted to shift the discussion back to the pilot again.

"Showin' off, if you ask me. Like always," she said.

"How's that?" Mitch asked.

"Oh he does this weird kind a airplane thing all the time. He claims it's a training maneuver. He shuts off the engine. The propellers stop spinning.

He floats for a spell. And then when it goes into a dive, it's supposed to somehow crank up again."

"Who's he showin' off for?" he asked.

Lady A didn't say anything at first. "I reckon it didn't crank up like it always does. So there you go."

Before Mitch could follow up, a huge black pickup truck pulled up behind them and groaned to a stop. All the windows were tinted, and the exterior had a gun-barrel-black gleam. It was jacked up and sitting on top of customized wheels and rims. The truck tipped sideways, and a very large man oozed out of the driver's side and thumped onto the ground. He was wearing leather driving gloves and an orange baseball cap. He wasted no time tromping into the middle of their conversation, where he stopped and turned his chest toward the burning dance barn. "Name's Gilreath, ladies and gentleman. Berry damn Gilreath, in case you are a snake reporter or some similar creature. Who is the unfortunate owner of that disabled crop duster?"

Mitch could hear the man's patchy breathing, and it sounded as if he was grappling for air to pull out every word.

"Hey, Berry. Over here. It's me, Amelia Stone." She pointed to Mitch, but Berry Gilreath turned and interrupted.

"Yes, Miss Lady A, the queen of the petites. Lovely as always, despite your cloak of dissheveledness. And I know who *that* is…we went to school together…your family moved…ah, the interloper. You have engaged in asking about the unfortunate demise of Myron and Lori Leigh? Right? You are the very squeak whom I seek. We need to converse."

Mitch saw that the man's jumbo jeans were landsliding in the back. Suddenly, without any hint of his earlier dignity, Gilreath went into a crab walk, rocking from side to side. He hooked his fingers into the belt loops and struggled to yank his jeans at least partially above his belly. The man walked out a few more steps toward Scuffletown and pointed to the burning dance barn. "The gods of calamity, for damn well once in the history of the Gilreath dynasty…have finally missed their intended mark."

Gilreath's statement about wanting a meeting made Mitch a little uneasy. "Berry, I was already lookin' to meet with you. Talk about your lawsuit...you and Reames."

"About what, and why?" Gilreath inhaled deep and long, removed his cap, and slapped it across his thigh.

"He's got a show on TV...that's why," Lady A said.

"Well..." Gilreath started and stopped. "Let's see if we can get all this riffraff to clear out, and then we can conference. What show?"

Mitch began to explain, but Gilreath held up both hands and twisted back to face the burning building.

"Right now...I just want to abide here in silence for a spell. Savor my good fortune. Don't misjudge me. The untimely loss of life and limb arising from an aeronautic tragedy...that is not the proper occasion to engage in celebratory hoopla. But gaze, if you will, upon that smoky entanglement. For once...it's not emanating from the Gilreath side of this godforsaken road. What a *di*-vine difference a property line makes."

"When you want to get together?" Mitch asked with confidence.

"Mister Beam...be kind enough to postpone our legal rendezvous for at least twenty-four hours. Here's my card."

As Mitch allowed the entire encounter to sink in, he couldn't take his eyes away from the corn silk sprouts flaring out from the rims of Gilreath's ball cap. Without any warning, Gilreath opened his arms, and to Mitch it looked as if the man were trying to embrace the entire landscape. When Gilreath finally lowered his arms and shuffled back toward his truck, Mitch spotted in the distance the creeping movements of Bud Culdock's T-Bird taxi. It was twenty cars or so farther back in the stalled and agitated traffic. In that moment, Mitch realized for certain that he was witnessing but not completely understanding the drawing power of turbulent light.

———

After the remnants of the fire were finished off, a burnt smell had attached itself to everything. Firemen entered what was left of the dance barn and doused and poked at a handful of hot spots. Chief Swanger and his deputies restored the traffic flow on Scuffletown Road, and Mitch offered to drive Lady A back to her shop, which was only about a mile away.

Somehow along the way, he primed up enough courage and stumbled out enough clues from gulped half sentences to inform her that he was attempting to ask her out for some kind of a date. She accepted with a handshake just as Mitch pulled his Cutlass Supreme up in front of her shop. She opened and closed the door so gently it didn't make a sound. She waved, and the air whooshed back at him and carried what remained of her perfume diminished by rain, fire smoke, getting buried by a quilt, winning a fistfight with two women, and rolling in mud and wet grass. Mitch sat for a few minutes to try to backtrack on what he had just done.

When Lady A slipped into her Mustang and then drove off, he cranked up again and turned off the radio, and after a few of miles of thinking about Lady A, his thoughts somehow locked onto the enigmatic Bud Culdock and the story of the shoe-shop taxi man.

CHAPTER 29

Culdock's Sole Music was the only shoe-repair business within twenty miles of Fountainville. Its lower roof line stood stark beside the three-storied James Furniture Store on one side and Gallman Drug Store's two-story, all-glass front on the other. The shoe shop had a tan brick veneer street side, and the wrinkled awning anchored to the roof above it gave the look of a loosely fitting gaberdine raincoat. Something a divorce lawyer's private eye might wear.

Many in the town believed that the gap created by the shoe shop's lower roofline was ideal for accommodating the black clouds that perpetually hovered above the life of its owner, Bud Culdock.

—

When the structure was constructed following World War II, it opened up as Roberson's Hardware Store. When Stan Roberson died of cancer, his widow moved away and sold it to Bobby Tinsley, who ran Tinsley's Family Jewelry Store out of it for the next fifteen years. When Tinsley retired, the rest of the family abandoned the jewelry trade and went their different ways. For a handful of years, Tinsley leased it to the Masons Lodge 73. The Masons vacated when they found another windowless warehouse just outside town. That left the building without any tenant and vacant for about a year and a half until the midsixties, when Kool-Daddy's Pool Parlor bought it to become the first African American commercial establishment on Main Street. For several years the pool hall flourished as a perfect commercial neighbor.

Following the integration of the Greenville County schools, however, Kool-Daddy's became the site for a series of Saturday-night knife- and fistfights. The owner, Benny Barksdale, eventually became entangled in a flurry of civil lawsuits based on the negligence theory that he had failed to provide adequate security and a safe premises for his patrons. It was inevitable that Barksdale would fall on hard times. Chief Cat Swanger then piled on when he busted him for illegal gambling and running parlay cards, forcing the Tinsley Family to evict him. The elimination of the popular hangout and its proprietor set off a six-month race boycott of downtown businesses.

Then, in the mid-1970s, the economy tanked. Real estate investment and sales fell victim to escalated interest rates forcing large numbers of bankruptcies and foreclosures.

Out of that financial maelstrom, Bud Culdock, who was still recovering from his criminal trial and miraculous acquittal for killing his wife's lover, swooped in with a mysterious wad of cash and bought the building at a foreclosure sale. He got it for practically nothing.

Culdock tried to score some goodwill points by donating Kool-Daddy's pool tables, barstools, and other furniture to the Fountainville Youth Recreation Center, Trinity Methodist Church, and Fountainville First Presbyterian. Before the pool tables were moved, both congregations united for a single outside service at Fountainville High football stadium. The service featured preachers who had unique ways of praying away evil spirits, invoking hedges of protection supplied by cherubim and seraphim, and blessing and dedicating all future billiard activity to racial harmony and spreading and demonstrating the Good News.

Culdock's commercial plans for the building teetered between launching the town's first dry-cleaning business or opening up a shoe shop. He had grown up learning a few things about shoe and leather repair from his father, who moonlighted by patching and restoring leather. Culdock opted for the shoe-shop route when he discovered the high cost of purchasing and maintaining dry-cleaning equipment. His second source of income was going to be a taxi service.

When the grand opening date for Culdock's Sole Music came around, it rained steadily all day. Mayor Gil Stoddard delivered extended remarks interspersed with a chain of shoe puns for the benefit of a smattering of five or six dedicated chamber of commerce members.

Later, the mayor and Bud Culdock collaborated to hold up a pair of oversized scissors to cut the grand opening ribbon. The mayor's wife, Desiree, was all decked out in spiked heels and a fur jacket and caused a commotion by stepping backward into a drainage grate. She toppled like a diseased pine and snapped both the ulna and radius bones in her arm so that her arm swung freely like a limp flag. There was chatter about a lawsuit against the town, but the mayor pulled the plug real quickly after his political advisers explained the political downside of suing his own town.

CHAPTER 30

The night after the fire brought Fountainville the first measure of coolness between summer and fall, and clouds soundlessly swept in along with their travel bags of light rain and scattered breeze. Mitch could almost hear the older pine needles letting loose and tick-ticking onto the tin roof of A.P.'s farmhouse. The remnant smoke from the banner plane crash had dispersed a confusing smell that to Mitch Beam's aroma memory seemed like a mix of burnt oil and wet leaves. Even as Mitch sipped his coffee, yesterday's air blunted the coffee taste.

A.P. had written a note earlier that morning about leaving town for about a week to meet a contractor to work up a quote for plumbing another bank building and maybe a couple of motels.

They didn't get the chance to hash out the Scuffletown excitement from the day before. Mitch cradled his cup, warm and comforting to his hands and fingers. He began to think about his return to Fountainville. So far, it had proven to be a mixed bag of jump-starting his troller career with cases to sell to *The Judge Smack Jack Show*. It also set off a series of intriguing tussles with old friends and fragments of memories. He had somehow even gotten himself a date with an old crush. As he wrestled with the pros and cons of staying in Fountainville or leaving, he thought about the characters and the stories of the place and how they fed his soul like a hot bowl of grits loaded with cheddar cheese, butter, and salt.

Even though the angst of Scuffletown Road was as bewildering and smouldery as ever, he was determined to continue trolling and stay long enough to satisfy the curiosities that had lured him to stay for a spell.

CHAPTER 31

Up in the Sanctified Hill part of town at Sharona Riddle's Pink House, Sweetie Bates unhooked the screen door by feel with her back turned. She used her hip to bump-squeak the springs a few times while she swung a broom at a moth to swat it outside. The door flapped back into place, and she stood there for a few seconds. She could have been a Yankee soldier at the end of a skirmish awaiting a surefire counterattack. "Miss Sharona...is it gonna stay cold this time?"

"You lookin'...out that back door again?" Sharona Riddle's voice barely had enough steam to push out a few words at a time. "No one knows..." she started and then said no more.

Sweetie took it from there. "Nobody knows what day or hour...I know all that...I'm just talkin' about winter. That's all," she mumbled.

"Sweetie? Sweetie...I had me another dream last night. Even wrote a poem. Get on back here."

Sweetie started walking toward Miss Sharona's room. "Yes, ma'am. Now you know...watch ya blood pressure. Ain't a doctor in this town gonna drop no golf game for nobody. Specially on a weekend." Sweetie sat down next to Sharona's bed and picked up the slack in the oxygen tube. "Now, let's hear it."

Miss Sharona closed her eyes. "I don't recall *all* the particulars. It came on...right before I woke. I just know...somethin's about to happen. We 'bout to have us a guest to get ready for. And I got all that Myron-and-Lori Leigh stuff brewing up, just a janglin' my thoughts."

"Oh no. It ain't that Mitch man, is it?" Sweetie said and repositioned herself in her chair.

"No...no...it's somebody good. And...just so you know, it ain't my death, angel...it's somebody good." Miss Sharona opened her eyes again and smiled.

"Well then, I got to finish all this paperwork." Sweetie held out her medical chart notebook high enough for Miss Sharona to see. "I got to check your vitals...about three days' worth."

"Don't you waste...one more speck a precious time...on all that. You see...in my dream, I had me these two huge pots a mixed flowers...at the back door...They were spectacular. Indigos...blue azure...a little bit a fern thrown in...red salvia...but the centerpiece was my fave...the most gorgeous purple irises. Oh, you should a seen it, Sweetie."

"Miss Sharona...you know I don't know nothing 'bout flowers. No ma'am. That ain't my gift." Sweetie pulled out her blood-pressure cuff.

"Sweetie, in my dream I had visitors...I couldn't see their faces, but I heard their voices...they were ones I knew...They took one look at my flowers...and they just went on and on. 'Inspirin''...that's the word they kept sayin'."

"It's just 'cause you like flowers." Sweetie began making notes in her medical chart. "Now, let me see that arm. Take your blood pressure."

"See here, Sweetie...flowers were made as gifts to make somebody's day...and it's all a part a God's plan...to time those flowers...just when somebody needs 'em...God knows..."

Sweetie suddenly jumped to her feet and reached and swung her cupped hand, first to the left, then toward the floor. "There's another one. Where are they comin' from?" She swiped a wash cloth from the top of the bedside table and snap-popped at another moth, which left a powdery trail. It sputtered and flew in a wide circle, dove, careened, and then disappeared through a gap in the blinds. "Oh, he just wants the light...and get gone."

"Sweetie...you 'bout to have a spell...hear me now. Forget that bug. I want you to get me two pots...and a nice mix a colors. You get a real florist...if you need it."

"Now, Miss Sharona, don't make me do no flowers. I get all sniffly. And anyway, they just die," Sweetie said and folded her arms.

"By their flowers ye shall know them. That's what I say," Sharona said. "And that's what they said in my dream three times...and that's when I heard this bang like a pistol shot...my dream, my wonderful dream... sailed away...and then it floated on down the Enoree.

"Now, tell me what you think about what I just wrote. It just came to me. Just as soon as I got through with that dream." Sharona reached into her robe pocket, pulled out an envelope, and unfolded it. "Sweetie, go on now. Have a seat." Sharona Riddle adjusted her pillow behind her and pushed her glasses farther up the bridge of her nose. "Here goes."

The Irises of Sanctified Hill

Peels of blue swords
Spray from a single shoot.
And a sheath
Gives way and barely holds
Against a nearby storm
Flipping the higher leaves.
A gold water bucket
In a tuft of weeds
Has tipped
And lies a few steps away,
Showing its underside
And a bullet hole.

"Flowers, bucket, and a bullet hole." Sweetie weighed in a few seconds after Miss Sharona finished reading. "That's all I got from it."

CHAPTER 32

Over the next two days, Mitch made another visit to the magistrate's court to meet with Kathy Moss. She gave him all the information she had on the new case, including how to contact the defendant, Samp Reames. "Mitch Beam…" Kathy Moss cleared her throat. "Don't ever turn ya back on a preacher man. Especially one that's a horse trader. Who cusses like a sailor."

"How 'bout I use your phone?" he asked with some hesitation. "If he answers, I might have to get you to grease the skids with him."

"Aw, Samp's okay. He'll meet with ya. When you say something about money, he'll prob'ly jump all over it. But for every word comes out a that mouth, remember: grain a salt. And keep your eyes *full* wide open." She clapped her hands three times. "Come on now. Go on and call. Your real tough nut's gonna be Gilreath anyway. Come on and get this easy one out the way."

Mitch got lucky and connected with Reames on the first call, and they set up a meeting for lunchtime at the Reames farm. Mitch thought that Reames was crunching potato chips during the whole conversation, and the directions were a little sketchy. Kathy Moss drew him a map on the back of a flyer for Bucky's Bonds—*You Ring, We Spring*. "You can't miss it if you know whatcha lookin' for."

Mitch drove by the unmarked drive twice, but when he passed the Enoree River Bridge rail a third time, he barely caught sight of a horsehead-shaped mailbox. It was tucked into the shadowy bend of a dirt drive.

He came to a stop and peered into the heart of the trees as best he could. He made a sharp turn into the drive and immediately clunked his front tires squarely into a succession of bucket-size potholes all hidden by tree shade. Along the ridge of the Enoree River, trellis after trellis of muscadine vines fanned out across rolling pastureland on both sides of the drive all the way out to the horizon. When he had traveled about fifty yards from the main road, the dirt drive became smooth asphalt, and he drove quietly and slowly along for about a half mile until the drive topped a hill and then angled back down toward the river. From that spot he finally saw Reames's farmhouse. It looked to Mitch as if it lay on its haunches guarding the property like the Great Sphinx of Giza.

The front door whooshed as soon as Mitch placed his finger on the door bell. A man stepped forward and filled up the open doorframe. Right through the gap under Reames's armpits, Mitch saw a blazing fireplace. That blast of heat and the intensity of the man's stare provided Mitch a gravity storm that wobbled him as he followed the man inside toward the fireplace. After a few steps, Mrs. Gwynne Reames, Samp's second wife, popped into view out in front of her giant husband. Mitch stopped walking, and she spoke.

"Mistuh Beam, I understand? I know your mama and daddy. I hate that they moved." Gwynne Reames was a petite woman. She weighed eighty pounds tops. The eyelid over her left eye seemed to hang like a broken curtain. She wore a full-length kind of a dress that could be worn at a high-occasion reception or cocktail party. Samp, by contrast, wore a pair of work boots caked with old mud and a sweatshirt emblazoned with the logo from his Enoree Hunt Club. Mitch couldn't help staring at Reames's hair. It sprang from two clusters, and the longer strands lopped over two hardpan bald spots like spooked birds dodging buckshot.

"Cocola, Mr. Beam?" Mrs. Reames asked. "Please let me serve you a Cocola. We have so many. Don't know what to do with them. And they're every one nicely chilled for our before-five-o'clock guests." She scampered off without waiting for Mitch to answer.

"So…" Samp started and collapsed full weight into an oversized recliner. He waved palm down, and Mitch sat in the only other chair, a recliner, much smaller, on the other side of what looked to be a den adorned with a fully stocked bar and fireplace.

Mitch waited several seconds, and the pressure of silence, which he hated more than anything, squeezed him into finally speaking. "Mr. Reames…"

"Please don't ever call me 'Mistuh'. Makes me want to keep a gimlet eye out for my daddy. Meanest son of a bitch ever breathed air. Anyway, go on. Tell me. Why you so interested in this little legal war we whipped up around here?"

Mitch launched into his role as a troller for *The Judge Smack Jack Show*. And he explained how the parties stood to make some money if his boss thought the case was unique enough to tantalize the audience.

Before Mitch could delve further into the contractual details and obligations, Reames slapped both palms against the chair arms. "Well, that arrogant jackass sued me first. *He* sued *me*! And there he was, Mr. Copperhead. All down in the pine needles. Trying to lie me into paying for a stud horse. With thoroughbred bloodlines. Showed me his stud book and all the tailines."

"Mr. Samp…" Mitch felt the overloaded Reames transfer truck was building up too much speed for the fast-approaching next curve.

In perfect timing, Gwynne Reames returned to the den. The tiny tray was crammed with a Coke bottle, a glass of ice, and a shot glass touching and rattling on each of her tiny steps. "Nice refreshment for our guest and my Samp. Gettin' down to business, I hope…dear."

Mitch poured his Coke into his glass of ice, and the fizz crept above the rim but didn't leak over. He looked up as soon as the Coke level dropped and saw Samp Reames throw back whatever was in that shot glass.

"Mr. Beam." Gwynne Reames took hold of the empty shot glass and spoke up. "That's my Samp's afternoon medicine. A calm set of nerves makes our world peaceful. It won't be long till he's ready for a happy nappy. Now, please carry on while the time is ripe."

"Mr. Samp, how come he—" Mitch got part of his question out and then sat back a little when Samp interrupted.

"I know whatchoo gonna ask just as sure as the world." Mitch studied Reames, who closed his eyes and smiled. "Well…I might a been wearing a slight disguise. Wig and mustache was all. And then I got to thinkin' I might just be able to pull one over on who I was. See, it was gettin' kind a dark. It started out being halfway for fun for me, at least until I perceived that he was full bore tryin' to dupe me. And then that just sort a pissed me off."

"I think I'll step out now." Gwynne Reames gathered the two glass-es and exited, humming what sounded to Mitch like "Onward *Christian Soldiers*."

Samp Reames whoomped himself forward in his recliner so that his feet touched flat to the floor. To Mitch, Reames looked like he was an of-fensive guard bracing to pass block. He faced Mitch and stared for a few seconds. "You see, I looked over his horse for a bit when I got there. I had a hunch he still had some stud life left in him. That horse was just plain ol' garden-variety depressed. And since I had the old son of a bitch on a line, I went on and played him some slack. I said, 'Well, I'm really just looking for a riding horse for my granddaughter. Not a famous race horse. You got something like that?'"

"What did Gilreath do then?" Mitch asked and took one more swig of Coke.

"He said something like, 'Well, I tell you what.' And then is when I knew he was probably wantin' like hell to sell that sad-sack stud that he believed was dried up. He put on quite a show, walkin' around him, pattin' him down. He even made it look like he was choking up. Like selling him was gonna be like putting him down or something."

"And you knew, but he didn't," Mitch said and then waited for the rest of the story. "Horse-tradin' at night, huh?"

"It's like this, troller man." Reames hesitated for a few seconds. "If you live too close to a waterfall, you get to where you can't hear it."

"But go on and tell how it got to be a lawsuit," Mitch said to prime the pump for more of the story.

"After I bought him, a couple a years went by, and next thing you know, my new horse has got himself some new surroundings. Got himself undepressed, and he starts to stud up a storm. And somehow, word just got out." Reames laughed until he snorted.

"So I read the complaint. He sued you for fraud, right?" Mitch saw Reames close his eyes, and he wondered about the onset of the happy nappy. "Mr. Samp!"

"Yeah." His eyes popped open. "But then my lawyer went and one-upped their ass. We counterclaimed 'em for what my lawyer called 'superseding fraud.' The way he explained it in lawyer talk was that even though we might a been committin' fraud, which I just call plain ol' horse-tradin', Gilreath's fraud was worsen what we did. As the lawyer explained, since Gilreath's fraud started before ours did, it 'superseded' whatever we were doin'. So we counterclaimed their ass. Best de-fense is damn good offense."

"Man, this is just great. I like the hell out of this whole story. It's got some show power. Now, you willing to sign up for the show? I'm telling you, I think they'll eat this thing up." Mitch presented the pen and the contract to Reames, who twirled the pen and held the contract in his lap. He leaned back and closed his eyes.

"Mr. Samp? It could be some good money."

"I'm prayin', son." Reames closed his eyes again. After a few seconds, he held up the contract, laid it across his face, and began to speak. Mitch could see Reames's lips trembling the paper, but he couldn't make out anything Reames was saying.

"Mr. Samp, make sure you read it. One thing to remember. You get paid, win or lose." Mitch knew the case had good show possibilities. He could almost see his commission check sliding into his wallet.

"I already know what's in this thing, brother. I'll sign, but Gilreath ain't gonna like it. Not one bit. He's likely not to go along with it. I bet when you go to him, he's gonna have something up his sleeve."

As soon as Reames finished signing, Mitch grabbed the contract and headed to the door. "Pray for me, Mr. Samp. I'm goin' to Gilreath. And thank Mrs. Gwynne for that Cocola."

CHAPTER 33

Mitch spun out when he left Samp Reames's farmhouse, wheeling away from the Enoree River and down onto the dirt stretch that connected Scuffletown Road. He came to a stop and couldn't see a thing and waited for the dust to settle. Berry Gilreath had said he'd be waiting to meet with him around one o'clock. Mitch had made good time with Samp Reames and was only a ten-minute ride from Gilreath Farms. He was part giddy but also part anxious about how Gilreath would react. His hands began to sweat on the wheel when he realized he hadn't really mapped out how to jump-start the meeting with Gilreath. His thoughts jumbled.

As he neared the Gilreath Farm gate, he couldn't help but think about the unusual nature of the Gilreath versus Reames case, but also about Myron's GTO, Lori Leigh, and Billy. He looked over again at the signature page and wondered if he could ever persuade Gilreath to sign.

Mitch was surprised to find the gate completely open. A short distance up the inclined drive, Gilreath's black truck was slunked over the left edge and partly on the grass, which was thick and rain-rich green. As Mitch slowed his Cutlass and turned in, a small smoke cloud banked above the obscured side of the truck. He stopped and looked in all directions for Berry Gilreath but saw nothing.

In a few seconds, he watched the angle of the truck even out, and then a door slammed. Berry Gilreath moseyed from behind the truck, stopped, and waved. He was smoking the fattest cigar Mitch had ever seen, and its smoke trailed from Gilreath's oversized safari hat all the way back to the larger cloud above the truck. To Mitch it looked as if Gilreath was waving for him to come over.

"Mr. Berry Gilreath?" Mitch asked even though he knew who was underneath the hat. He didn't know whether to start formal or friendly. "I'm Mitch Beam. We met the other day when the banner plane crashed. Amelia Stone introduced us."

Gilreath puffed on the cigar a few times. "I recall our brief and muddled encounter, sir." Gilreath pulled his cigar out of his mouth, flicked the ashes, and spewed a smaller smoke stream from the corner of his mouth. "I remember being swept up in a catastrophe that evolved rather instantaneously, at least from my perspective, into a tumult of pure ecstasy. But yes, I do recall our brief social intercourse. So…why? Why are you so… captivated by my litigation with my lifelong nemesis, the veritable thorn in my flesh?"

Mitch stepped forward and presented him the contract. He spoke quickly, describing his job as a troller for *The Judge Smack Show* and how both parties would reap the benefit of being paid. He also explained how he had already spoken to Samp Reames and obtained his signature.

"So, tell me, Mr. Professional Scab Picker, why did you first approach Samp the snake handler? I do believe he's a practicer in the Free Will Baptist cult."

Mitch didn't hesitate. "Because I knew that you would see the positive upside to signing up on the case. I knew that only you had the sophistication and savvy to discern a good business opportunity when you saw one. And two…well, poor Mr. Reames, he might be good with disguises, but when it comes to something like goodwill or reputation, his cupcake ain't got as much icing."

Gilreath chuckled, and Mitch squinted, pursed his lips, and locked his jaw to make Gilreath believe his sincerity.

"Mr. Beam," Gilreath said and then puffed his cigar and removed it to flick the ashes again. "If you truly believe I'm as sapient as you so generously profess, then why would you think I would drop a clanger over that stream of—excuse this scatological reference—squirrel squirt?"

Mitch locked in on Gilreath's eyes, but he was buying some time as he struggled with Gilreath's vocabulary. "I don't chew my butter beans but once, Berry Gilreath. You're smart enough to know it's a good deal for your purposes." Mitch cleared his throat to hide a huge gulp.

Gilreath turned, took a few steps up his drive, and stopped. "So why do you believe I commenced this lawsuit against the Reverenced Samp Reames?"

"I know for sure one thing." Mitch walked far enough up the hill so he could be certain Gilreath could hear him and see his face. "It damn sure wasn't for money. You filed your case in the magistrate's court. Small claims court. Low jurisdictional cap. So damages ain't your real goal. Right?"

"Go on, then," Gilreath said and drew on his cigar again.

"I think this is all about pride. Savin' face in the racehorse community. Rep-you-tay-shun. Nailed it, didn't I?" Mitch threw everything to the wind and waited, expecting the worst.

Gilreath chuckled louder and longer this time. "You mind if we sit in your Oldsmobile Cutlass for a spell, Mr. Beam? Okay to smoke?"

"Sure. I might crack the window though."

"The timing and context of your humor, Mr. Beam, is extraordinary. And, I might add, rather dark, taking into account our tragic setting. I appreciate it though. And by the way, you and the Cole Boy who recently expired...y'all were childhood friends, were you not?"

Once the two of them were seated in the car, Gilreath immediately rolled down his window. Mitch cranked up, turned on the air, and placed the contract and pen in Gilreath's lap. While he waited on Gilreath's response, he thought about Gilreath's random question about Billy.

"So, as a preamble, would you be kind enough to recount for me what Reverend Serpent whispered to you in his riverside snake den?" Gilreath blew a stream of smoke through the window and started speaking again before Mitch could say anything. "In my world, you must have some degree of prescience to see that when it comes to a cheating horse trader—and that's not redundant, Mr. Troller Man—the whole world exists on the tip of the tongue."

Mitch read partly from his notes and filled in additional puzzle pieces with the other things he remembered from his Samp Reames meeting.

"I see, said the blind man," Gilreath said and sat silently for about a minute. "I very much esteem your unsolicited candor, Troller Man."

"If you want to give your version…" Mitch barely cracked the lid, and Gilreath flew out.

"Tip of the hat, sir, for your latitude of my expression." Gilreath cleared his throat. "My treasured racehorse, the one and only Fabulous Malochi, had not sired anything for…well, about a year. I frankly inferred that he was expended as a stud. But, in light of his registry, tailine, and racing record prowess, I surmised his remnant of stature and notability. I envisioned capitalizing upon my financial advantage. So I arranged for the word to be disseminated. In your words, I 'put out feelers.'" Gilreath rolled down the window and spit out a string of tobacco.

"Well that's kind a what Reames alleged," Mitch said. "It's all in his pleading. He calls it the 'start of the defrauding.'" Mitch stopped and waited for Gilreath to respond.

"I may have been a skosh short of a full and complete disclosure concerning Malochi's potential impotence." Gilreath stopped and closed his eyes. "In view of your lexicon, Mr. Beam, I acknowledge to being a little 'loosey-goosey' about the stud history."

"The way I heard it, Reames flat out duped ya…and with nothin' but a cheap disguise?" Mitch asked to try to squeeze more out of the toothpaste tube.

"Yes…I acknowledge that, to some degree," Gilreath said. "The snake in the grass did prove to be Mr. Reames. I was not as vigilant as I should have been."

"And all of it took place face-to-face?" Mitch asked.

"Despite your previous characterization of the quality and price of his disguise, I deemed it to be somewhat professional as a disguise," Gilreath said. "Efficacious for sure. And do not overlook this factor: Reames manifested before me in the lightless portion of the evening."

"At night?" Mitch asked.

"And at his persistence of inquiry, I acknowledged my possession of a racehorse stud. I did disclose that Malochi had not studded out in a while," Gilreath said. "And that's when he set the trap for me. He said, 'All I really need is a riding horse for my granddaughter.' All of that, we know by way of hindsight, was his verbal trickery to drive down my asking price."

"Riding horse?" Mitch asked.

"But being somewhat gifted with agility of the mind, I proceeded to toss him a price on Malochi that was lower than stud price. But higher than a riding horse," Gilreath said.

"So it was some back-and-forth between y'all?" Mitch asked.

"Here, Mr. Beam, is the rather *sui generis* dilemma placed before me." Gilreath stopped. "I needed to sell that horse due to financial pressures. And the pressures were mounting due to the weight of our tainted land. I didn't want to carelessly expend an offer on the horse. So in the course of our negotiations, I reduced the price accordingly. I had no particle of evidence that Lucifer Reames knew Malochi's true veterinary condition."

"So…Reames…he had…" Mitch started, but Gilreath jumped in.

"Reames had veterinary training, and he fraudulently withheld information of Malochi's curable condition from me," Gilreath said. "Mr. Beam, I am becoming quite proficient in this role of spoon-feeding."

Mitch tapped his pen on his notepad. "So how'd it happen that you heard about Malochi's stud comeback?"

"I heard from an array of sources." Gilreath flicked his half-smoked cigar into the thick grass. It sent a trail of smoke for a few minutes. He remained silent. "I knew that I would have to litigate to get the full story out there. Fortify against the potential sabotage of my reputation as a horseman. Seemed logical. Gossip had it that I was duped into an unbalanced transaction."

Mitch saw that Gilreath was beginning to look like a flat tire. "So, you 'bout ready to sign?" Mitch said quickly.

"Possibly," Gilreath whispered. And then he sat up straight and rubbed his hands as if he were trying to spark a flame. "However…I've got some conditions. We need to discuss those before we can move forward. Step over here and stroll with me for a spell."

"Yes sir, I can do that. And just so you recall, I already got Reames to sign on."

"Splendid," said Gilreath. "I do recall that revelation."

Mitch got out and followed Gilreath for about the length of a football field, until Gilreath stopped and lowered himself onto the trunk of crooked oak that ran parallel to the ground. A perfect bench. Gilreath was breathing heavily, and his cheeks were watermelon red.

"I know that you have been interrogating some of my fellow Fountainvillians about Myron Parsons and Lori Leigh Cole. You are resurrecting some buried pain about our beloved teenagers." Gilreath motioned for Mitch to join him on the oak perch. Gilreath pulled his safari hat over his forehead so that it left part of his face in the shadows.

"I have been," Mitch said. "I see a possible story for me. Possible one. It's what I do. That's all it is."

"Are you familiar with the word 'tainted'?" Gilreath asked. "I'm confining the employment of that term to the context of real estate sales."

"I suppose," Mitch said.

"My family land here that I'm struggling to market," Gilreath started. "It has been forever plunged into a morass of taint for almost two centuries. Surely you have heard the legend about the apparition of Benjamin Stairley? Well, that bogus ghost tale has tormented our land with a cloud of taint ever since my family bought a section of the Stairley plantation from Stairley's estate. The story goes that when Stairley was tortured and killed by Sherman's troops, one horse ran up Scuffletown Road scattering parts of his anatomy all over Scuffletown. And sometimes, especially when the moon is full, Stairley's ghost is supposed to stalk the countryside searching for his lost body parts."

"I remember some a that," Mitch said.

"Land loaded down with taint will not market well. Ghosts, we have learned, are the worst forms of taint," Gilreath said. "And then, in 1975, we had the deaths of those beloved teenagers. By pure happenstance, they died on our land. Barely. Right over there. But barely is all it takes. You can see the very spot. I had it bulldozed. Removed every vestige of the event. Occasionally, I called the law on curiosity seekers, vandals, and whatnot.

And you know what? Real estate taint apparently has a thousand lives. Nobody wants to buy that kind of real estate."

"Never looked at it that way," Mitch said.

"Now, we enjoyed an unexpected turn of events the other day on that plane crash," Gilreath said. "Taint, you could say, finally had its spots knocked off."

"But then out of nowhere, here comes the Troller Man Mitch Beam. How does the Bard say it? 'No man's pie is freed from his ambitious finger.' Yes, here comes Mitch Beam exhuming Mr. Taint from his shallow grave." Gilreath stopped. His breathing was heavy. Sweat rilled from his forehead.

Mitch tried to defuse the man. "I didn't intend any a that."

"Here's the skinny, Mr. Beam. Again, I'm borrowing your vernacular. This information I am asking you now to hold in strict confidence. My family finally is finally poised to sell this property. All eighty-six acres. The closing is set one week from today. The buyer is some company out of New Jersey which apparently has not unearthed any of the taint of Gilreath Farms. They do not know about Stairley or Lori Leigh and Myron, or even vandalized signs. None of it. They want to develop a planned community right along Scuffletown. Our farm is the crown jewel. The whole community stands to reap revenue. *If*—if you can just have a brief cessation of your machinations about the dead teenagers until after the transaction has been completed, then—*then* I promise I will sign your TV contract for Gilreath versus Reames. In my analysis, everybody wins. What say you, Troller Man?"

Mitch sat and didn't say a word. He weighed the pros and the cons and grappled for the right response.

Gilreath was the first to speak up. "I see your cognitive machinery is accelerating in full motion. For the present circumstances, I will fold this contract for your TV show, and I will secure it in my papers. If you're okay with my proposal, then I promise I will sign it as soon as the closing is history. So?" Gilreath reached up as soon as Mitch rose, and Mitch pulled him to his feet.

"Yeah, I can wait on it. Let me know how the closing goes," Mitch said.

The two men shook hands, and Mitch walked back to his car and drove toward the front gate. As the vehicle tilted on the steepest part of the drive, a flash of afternoon sunlight bounced sharply off the mirror and into his eyes so that he was driving blind. He pressed the brake and put it in park. In that silent wait, he thought about the deal with Gilreath. Gilreath versus Reames. His instinct screamed to him that it was a real winner. That could mean a substantial paycheck. He blinked several times trying to wipe out the flash that continued to blur his vision. He knew with full certainty that he had no real choice but to wait out the seven days until the anticipated purchase of Gilreath Farms. He didn't know if he could hold off on talking about Myron and Lori Leigh. He also didn't know if he could fully trust Gilreath to sign the contract if he did.

When the sun spots dissolved, he saw that his front bumper was hanging partially over the edge of the road. Something made him look back. Gilreath was trying to walk downhill, doing his best tightrope act, side-stepping, digging in with his toes and the sides of his shoes, and flaring his arms for balance. He eventually found more level ground and lumbered all the way back to the oak-tree bench. He kicked and scraped some dirt and small rocks piled against the tree trunk. He hesitated, bent, and lifted a metal cover and pulled out another object covered with dirt and mud. To Mitch, it looked to have a kind of hinge in the middle. A chain dangled from one end. Gilreath held it for a few seconds and dropped it back into the ground. He replaced the cover and buried it again with the loose dirt and stones. Mitch slowly eased onto Scuffletown road, coasted for a bit, and then lightly accelerated back toward Fountainville.

Once Mitch had witnessed Gilreath unearthing the stick-like mechanism and then the reburial, he couldn't stop thinking about it. He rubbed his eyes and bore in with questions. What was it? Why was Gilreath so intrigued with it? And why did he discard it?

It was late in the afternoon when he decided to make his way back to A.P.'s farmhouse.

A.P. had left a morning message on the answering machine. He'd be back tomorrow. Mitch knew there was some catch-up cleaning to do. A.P. also said he'd be back in time for the Reverend Rooks hypnotist show.

Tomorrow was shaping into a jumbled mess. The hypnotist show and then the dessert-and-coffee date with Lady A. So what to wear to watch a hypnotist, he asked himself. He then wrestled with something somebody once told him about stage hypnotists. People in the audience can sometimes get hypnotized unwittingly. They end up doing all kinds of things.

PART V

CHAPTER 34

For over a month Fountainville had talked itself into something of an anticipation frenzy about the third day of October. It was either "Hypnotist" or "Evangelist" Day, depending on whether you identified as Methodist or Southern Baptist.

The autumn breeze on that crisp morning mostly slumbered, but occasionally it would throw a gust-punch like the one that lifted the oversized lid on Shelby Shillinglaw's Tupperware. Above her the branches of the oaks lining Main Street snare drummed in and out of rhythm.

For Shelby, it was a lung-stinging distance to walk from Sweet Shelby's all the way to the Sanctified Hill neighborhood. Standing there at the very front was the most prominent architectural feature in town, Sharona Riddle's Pink House.

When she successfully reached the front gate, she propped her shoulder there to catch her breath. "That is some kind a pink," she said to herself. As soon as she stepped onto the ramp, she noticed all the scripture burned into the planks. She took the time to stoop low enough to read each one. When she finally stood at the back door, traditionally Miss Sharona Riddle's love-potion-trading door, two black cauldrons posted on each side overwhelmed her and left little space to enter the door. Each was loaded with a color cascade of flowers and ferns.

As she tried to identify the different types of flowers and plants, the door swashelled like someone biting an apple. Shelby suddenly stood face-to-face with a wide-eyed Sweetie Bates.

"Miss Sharona…you ain't gonna believe what the wind done this time." She pushed out the screen door and hugged Shelby so hard the Tupperware lid flew completely off this time, and it sailed into one of the giant flower pots.

"Sweetie Bates, let me just look atchoo. You ain't changed a bit. With ya skinny nursing self."

"Miss Shelby, your eyes gettin' weak."

"So where is she? Can she eat my banana pudding?" Shelby asked and looked around the kitchen. "My secret recipe. I remembered how she loved it so, ever since we were little and my mama made it."

"She might be nappin', but let me put that in the fridge." Shelby watched Sweetie dig a spoon from a drawer and scoop a taste.

"Eatin' is the best compliment, Sweetie. So bless ya," Shelby said.

"Come on, lady, follow me," Sweetie said as she grabbed Shelby's hand and pulled her to Sharona's bedroom.

"My dream, Sweetie. I told ya it would be somebody good." Sharona Riddle unhooked herself from her oxygen tank and flung the tubes aside. She stayed seated but spread her arms wide.

Shelby took two steps and nudged Sharona so they could sit side by side. The two women just looked at each other, squeezed hands, and cried a good five minutes without saying a word. Sweetie left the room and came back with clutches of tissue.

"Sharona…those flowers. They just took my breath away."

"Me too," Sharona said and dangled her oxygen tubes until Shelby got the joke. And that set off another crying jag.

"I'm so sorry 'bout your Billy Boy…I know how you loved 'n prayed, loved 'n prayed," Sharona kept repeating until her voice gave way to a gasp. She put her tubes back in.

"We've been praying…since we were little. You'n me," Shelby said.

"Couldn't a made it one single day without my prayer warrior." Miss Sharona grabbed a tissue and dabbed a rill of tears on Shelby's cheek.

"He suffered so…but I knew…I felt your prayin'," Shelby said as she reached for Sharona's hand.

"I dreamed somebody was comin' to see me…I told Sweetie. I'm glad it was you."

"Guess what I brought? Just for my friend." Shelby got up, walked back to the kitchen, stacked three cereal bowls and spoons, returned, and placed the container gently onto Sharona's lap. "Throw off that lid see what it is," Shelby whispered.

"Oh, I know what that is." Sharona opened the container. "You didn't forget…you didn't forget. And I'm havin' some. So turn your head, sweetie-times."

"Just save me some." Sweetie laughed. "I'll grab us some tea."

For about an hour, the three of them stuffed themselves with banana pudding and tea, and they spun stories and laughed and cried over old times, and mostly they talked about people, but they also mixed in all kinds of solutions to problems, local, international, and even some that were biblical.

Once the three-engine time machine was just about out of time-travel fuel, Sharona pointed to Sweetie but took another shot of oxygen before she spoke. "I *do* love that red shirt on you, Sweetie. It's fine."

"Old lady, you must be wantin' more flowers, or something," Sweetie said.

"No, no, no. It's so red, it makes me wonder why we can't get a decent tomato. All summer long's what I'm sayin'." Sharona's voice was fading. "This year, nothing but green and yella. And hard as rocks."

"Now, Miss Sharona…" Sweetie crossed her arms and looked at Shelby. "You *do* know we done way past summer, right?"

Shelby sensed an awkward silence and jumped in to save Sharona any embarrassment. "There's absolutely nothing in this life, or maybe even when we're dancing on the streets of gold, that tastes as good as a summer tomato. You can't beat it. And throw in a little plop a Duke's on it, then some black pepper, and you gotta have Sunbeam bread. But you know what? And this is one of the great laws of nature. Even Duke's mayo can't save a green tomato," Shelby said, and all three clapped and a-menned and laughed some more.

"Yes, ma'am, you so right," Sharona added. "You can't redeem a green tomato."

When Sweetie gathered up all the bowls and spoons and started toward the kitchen, she turned back to them again. "I'm leavin' y'all's tea glasses in case ya want more. And now, I'm givin' y'all some private time."

"Friend a mine…" Shelby started to say, but when Sharona closed her eyes, she touched her hand to make sure she would hear what she came to say. "Friend, I've made this visit mainly just to give you some peace of mind."

"Peace I leave with you…my peace I give you…I do not give to you as the world gives…" Sharona said softly and gulped for more air. "Do not let your hearts be troubled…"

"And…" Shelby asked.

"Do not be afraid." Sharona finished the verse and stared at Shelby.

"That's a better way a sayin' what I'm here to tell you. And it's about the man that came out a nowhere to see you a month or so ago. He's scared to come back, but he wants to," Shelby said and dipped her head.

"If you referrin' to Mitch Beam the buzz killer, then don't say another word," Sharona said. "When he got to talkin' and brought up Myron, you know what came over me? It was the spirit of slap."

"We've had this talk before, my friend. Years ago. Nobody's blaming you one iota for Myron and Lori Leigh. I thought we already put all that behind us." Shelby clasped Sharona's hand that rested on top of her oxygen tank.

"Well, I thought I heard where he was goin'. I had a bad feelin'." Sharona opened her eyes wide and sat up straight. "Like I say, if you walkin' down a certain path, and you come up on a sharp curve, don't letcha feet touch the parts that ain't the path."

"Here's what you need to know. I don't want you sittin' up here frettin' about Mr. Mitch Beam. You know…it's like this. He works for a TV show. You probably watch it." Shelby stopped to try to gauge if Sharona was still listening.

"Which one?" Sharona asked.

"They call it *The Judge Smack Jack Show*," Shelby said and saw Sharona adjust herself in her recliner and take another sip of tea.

"So what's he wantin' with me?" Sharona asked.

"He's been told you're loaded with all kinds a stories, and not just the ones about Myron and Lori Leigh. He's wanting some of 'em to sell for that show. Here's what you need to know. If you can tell him something about that night, that's fine. Just know, he's lookin' at all the stories and rumors on what happened that night. But he ain't out to put the blame on you. He's lookin' at all kinds a stories around here."

Shelby finished and stood because her legs were falling asleep.

"That don't sound so bad," Sharona said.

"You give him a story he can use on the show, then you get paid for it," Shelby said. "Might mean a little extra spending money."

"Two six-packs was all Myron came for that night. And two of 'em's what he got. Just like always." Sharona's eyes shifted up toward where Shelby was sitting.

"We know that. That all came out," Shelby said to try to keep her talking and thinking.

"Chief told me...all my love potion was still in the bag. And all of 'em with the caps on too. They had nothin' to do with nothin'," Sharona said.

"Here's my solemn promise—and you know we go way back, right?" Shelby asked.

"Sure do."

"Even if you never say another word to mister Beam—or anyone else, for that matter—about that night, nobody's gonna put any blame on Sharona Riddle. Not on my watch," Shelby said. "We are prayer sisters, and you might even be my oldest living continuous friend. It's okay. Do not let your heart be troubled."

"Well..." Sharona started. "How you feel about a man calling hisself the evangelist hypnotist? Ain't that *in*-the-world and *of*-the-world teamin' up, kind a like?"

"Well, I confess. I'm gonna be there tonight with A.P., if you're askin' about if I'm going," Shelby said. "He's supposed to be back in time. Just barely."

"I just wouldn't want the Lord to come back while I was sittin' in on something like that." Sharona Riddle closed her eyes, and to Shelby it looked as if she might have fallen asleep.

Shelby kissed Sharona lightly on her forehead, and just as she was about to step out of the bedroom, she heard her old friend softly singing what sounded like a verse they sang together as children: "Do you know the muffler man, the muffler man, the muffler man? Do you know the muffler man, who lives on a Drury Lane?"

—

A couple of hours after Shelby departed, Sweetie brought Miss Sharona her late-morning decaf. She sipped on it for a few minutes until it was lukewarm. She balled up a napkin and stuffed it into the cup and handed it back to Sweetie.

"Sweetie...they's some folks thinking they got ab-so-*lute* power over me." Miss Sharona started shuffling her feet on the mat in front of her chair as if she were about to take off and fly. "But it ain't *real* power. The law ain't power. Money ain't power, not always. And some old nosey busy-body tryin' to put the blame on somebody. They might think *they* got the power. But...on Christ the solid rock I stand...all other ground is sinkin' sand...all other ground is sinkin' sand."

"You got that right, Miss Sharona," Sweetie said and handed her several pills. Miss Sharona dribbled a little water when she chased down her medicine. When she had regained her regular breathing, she turned to Sweetie. "Don't you forget...on my tombstone...I took love seriously. Don't forget to say that."

CHAPTER 35

When Mitch parked behind Sweet Shelby's, he thought he spotted Lady A's Mustang. He began the three-block walk toward James Furniture for the Reverend Jay Rooks Show. Fountainville First Baptist was the original venue because it had the largest seating capacity in town. It stayed set that way until a trio of vigilant deacons raised objections at a specially called church conference about the blatant intermingling of the secular dark art of hypnotism with the Great Commission art of evangelism.

The James family, all First Baptist members, heard about the controversy about using the sanctuary for the show. They immediately offered their furniture warehouse as an alternative site. The warehouse had its own platform stage and a sound system, and they often rented it out for estate auctions and social and community events such as piano and dance recitals, political rallies, and even wedding receptions whenever there were plans for serving alcohol or dancing.

Even after several months, the smoke odor from the dance barn fire seemed to Mitch as if it had been permanently painted in above the town, and when it rained, it would trowel into the shady streets and avenues.

He was a little early. After several false starts, he and Lady A agreed to the hypnotist show as their first date. They'd sit with A.P. and Shelby at the show, and then they'd follow with dessert and coffee at Sweet Shelby's. They were to meet up at the furniture store, and it was his job to find and hold four seats together.

While he was thinking about the fire smell and wrestling for a strategy to find four seats together, he almost tripped over what he thought at first might be a displaced mannequin from George's Men's Wear. They were always having clothes, mannequins, and even mannequins with the clothes still on shoplifted from their store and discarded. He regained his balance and stepped back over it and recognized that it was a real man in a suit. The man's upper torso was buried deeply into a row of boxwoods fronting the Gunn Funeral Home. The man had only one shoe and possibly a toupee. Those puzzle pieces instantly raised the red flag for Mitch on whether the outstretched man was dead or alive.

Mitch leaned into the bushes to find the man's face. The first thing he saw was a line of dried blood about the length of cattail caterpillar trailing from one of the man's nostrils. A pumpknot protruded from his cheek line. "Brother, you need some help? Sir...you okay?" Mitch implored.

The man's face and arms twitched, and then his legs began to roll side to side. He made sounds like a rusty well pump. The groaning lasted for about a minute. Mitch kept looking down both ends of the sidewalk hoping someone would come along to help him witness the spectacle. "Sir...sir...can I help you?" Mitch asked again. He glanced at his watch and knew he needed to get moving to the show.

The man sucked in some air, and his eyes flared. He reached out and clasped boxwood clumps in each hand and pulled up into a sitting position. More groaning. He looked at Mitch and lightly touched his swollen cheekbone. "Are you Fountainville Baptist?" the man asked.

Mitch gave the question some thought before responding. "Baptist...by curse, I guess. But Christian by choice." Mitch instantly felt guilty about his declaration and how it might be received at the heavenly gate.

"That's funny," the man responded. "It hurts to laugh, though." He completely grimaced his face into a walnut shell.

"Why you layin' in that bush, friend?" Mitch was compelled to seek a quick answer so he could continue on his way.

"Punched..." The man rubbed his cheek, which continued to swell and grow purple. "Let me ask you, friend...and thanks for stopping, by the way. Does everybody in this town just slug it out over everything?"

"It does prove to be quite a hobby for most. Truth is, we got us a slew a Scotch-Irish." Mitch felt compelled to be straight up with the stranger rather than to sugarcoat.

"I was walking along with somebody. Can't even say what the man looked like. I remember something was said about the hypnotist and the show, and I told him something like, did he know that only intelligent people can get hypnotized. Then, out of nowhere, whammo. I think I got knocked out, and I think he might have hit me with a sign of some kind."

"Who did it?" Mitch asked.

"Not a clue." After responding to Mitch's question, he broke several branches in a clumsy attempt to clamber out of the bushes. Mitch saw that the man had cuffed sleeves with gold cufflinks shaped like lightning bolts.

"You goin' to the show?" Mitch asked.

"Supposed to," the man said quickly. He slapped shrub parts off his suit and grunted on each movement.

"You could follow me. That's where I'm goin'. Would a been there by now, but I tripped over you. Sorry about that." Mitch gave him a hand sweep for him to come along, but the dazed man just stood there. Mitch reached for his wallet and pulled out a few dollars and pushed them into the stranger's hand. "Tell you what. You walk over to Sweet Shelby's restaurant. It's back that way next to the barber shop. You'll see the pole. It stays lit twenty-four-seven. Get cleaned up in the restroom. It stays clean. Buy ya some coffee and a slice a pie. If you want more, just tell 'em Mitch Beam said to put it on his bill. They'll do it."

"You didn't need to do all this," the stranger said.

"I frankly wish I could go with ya, stranger. Somehow I got hornswoggled into goin' to see this hypnotist. And on a first date too. God bless ya, friend." Mitch took off, and when he looked back, the punch-out victim continued to swat at his clothes. Mitch looked at his watch once more and increased his pace. Being late for his first real date with Lady A would be unfortunate. Failing to keep his promise to Shelby Shillinglaw to save four seats could be catastrophic.

About a block from James Furniture, men and women were marching in a line and carrying signs. He couldn't read them at first. In ten more paces, he could read them all: "HYPNOTISM ≠ EVANGELISM"; "SATAN'S SHOW," and "SIMON THE SORCERER." Then he recognized all the marchers. They were the entire twelve-man deacon body of Fountainville First Baptist Church. He speeded up into a trot so he could make it to the front doors before the line of protesters could loop back and block his path.

"Hey, hey, slow down, Richard Petty." A.P. Thackston's voice airhorned him into an instant stop. "The girls are savin' the seats." A.P. said and then spit a stream of tobacco juice into a cup. "I deserved another chew for comin' to this thing…and good news…we got time. Rusha's usherin'. Go ahead and give him a wave over there. He told me the hypnotist or preacher, or whatever he is, he ain't even here yet. They just had a guy announce it, so here I am. Lookin' out for your ass…once again."

"I knew Shelby'd wring my neck if I didn't get those seats," Mitch said, almost completely out of breath from a combination of run-walking and a healthy fear of Shelby Shillinglaw.

"Oh, they dragged me down here extra early. She predicted you'd be late. She called you on it. Come on, let's go." A.P. pulled Mitch with him into the furniture warehouse.

As they zipped through the warehouse crowd and closed in on the lighted platform, a man standing in the middle was making direct eye contact with Mitch. The man appeared to be studying the crowd. He cupped his hand over his eyes like he was looking for a late train to come chugging out of the fog. Mitch saw that the stage man's shirt also had big cuffs and gold lightning-bolt cufflinks.

Just then the lights dimmed, the crowd whooped, and Mitch and A.P. were forced to stop walking. Out of the dark, Lady A's hand reached up and pulled Mitch into his seat beside her.

"There you are, date. We just about to start…finally." Mitch couldn't see what she was wearing, which he was looking forward to, but he could see sparkles of patterns when she reached for him.

"Ladies and gentlemen," the man onstage began. But then he stopped to do a series of sound checks. "One, two, three…one, two, three…ladies and gentleman, there we go. I am Knox Gallman, and I'm Reverend Jay

Rooks's manager as well as the moderator for our event this evening. I am honored and pleased to inform you that Reverend Rooks has made it here, praise the Lord…and we have learned that he was delayed because he was in some kind of unfortunate accident. You'll see he's got a bump on his face. He's cleaning that up. He has asked me to pass along his sincere apology as well as his appreciation for your patience, which must be your town's spiritual gift. He is *not* one hundred percent, but he wants to go as long as he can. You are a blessing to him, and he wants to be a blessing to you. He covets your prayers for strength to share the message with you tonight. Now I'm getting a thumbs-up, so I present to you the most extraordinary evangelist in God's Milky Way…the Reverend Jay Rooks…"

After the applause erupted, Mitch watched a man limp onto the stage. It was the very man who had been punched and knocked deep into the bushes in front of the Gunn Funeral Home. Mitch leaned toward Lady A. "Remind me to tell you what I know about this guy."

The man needed some assistance from his manager to climb onto a stool. He took the microphone from Mr. Gallman, and he bowed his head until the clapping dissipated.

Lady A popped Mitch on the knee. "I've heard this man before. Maybe five, maybe six or seven years ago. Pretty sure it was in the sanctuary that time. Pretty sure he's the one. Don't you remember? Is that what you were gonna tell me?"

Mitch could see that she was getting a little worked up about it. "Maybe so. Yeah maybe so. Vaguely comin' back to me." Mitch answered that way hoping she'd settle down.

After considerable effort in mounting the stool, Reverend Rooks began to look uncomfortable on that perch. In a few seconds, he reversed course and slid gingerly away from it. When Mitch saw the way the seat tipped and spun, he knew it was one of the barstools that Bud Culdock had given away when he bought Kool-Daddy's. "Bad mojo on that thing," he thought.

"Let me open things up with a prayer, and then I want to speak with you a little bit about the book of Matthew. For those of you who brought Bibles and want to follow along, I use the NIV. Now please join me in a prayer of unity and peace, cleansing all the clutter of life's goings-on from our minds, souls, and spirits…"

As the speaker prayed, Mitch peeked left and right. Chief Swanger stood against a wall back in the corner, stage right and almost completely in the shadows. Mitch couldn't tell if Swanger's eyes were closed. He spotted Kathy Moss, Lady A's sister, and she had both hands raised. She occasionally piped up a "praise Lord" or an "amen" whenever Reverend Rooks took a breath. Hooks Hammond's son, Ricky, Billy Cole's best friend late in life, sat in the next section over, and he forgot to remove his cap for the prayer. Seeing Ricky reminded him that he had promised to go with Shelby whenever she decided to clean out Billy's shed. Reverend Rooks began evangelizing, and his voice was a rusty pulley. Mitch was already growing anxious about the hypnotism part.

"Now, brothers and sisters, thank you for just now interceding with me. You were interceding on behalf of this lovely community, her past and her future, and we know who holds the future, amen? A-men.

"Please stand with me while I read from your book of Matthew, chapter six, and your verses twenty-two and twenty-three. Follow along if you will.

"The eye is the lamp of the body. If your eyes are healthy, your whole body will be full of light. But…I say, *but* if your eyes are unhealthy, your whole body will be full of darkness. If…I say IF then the light within you is darkness, how great is that darkness! Amen? A-men." Reverend Rooks launched into the evangelism portion of the evening. He started off with a subdued tone and a slow cadence. Soon the volume escalated, and the rhythm accelerated, and thereafter he transported the audience onto an oratorical roller-coaster ride. Mitch's anxiety about the upcoming hypnotist time blocked out the substance of Reverend Rooks's sermon. The preacher ended with a benediction, and Mitch closed his eyes and tried to listen to the words.

"Now, my brothers and sisters, you have been evangelized. So…how about some fun and entertainment? Christians can have fun too. Amen? A-men."

Reverend Rooks stepped down from the stage and took several slow strides into the middle of the crowd. "From this very moment," he began and then paused. "Everything I say to you…every single thing I say, no matter how far-fetched or stupid it seems, will be the reality that you will be living in. Every single thing will become your world, your everything, and your reality, even if it seems outlandish. *Your* reality. Got it? I will start off by asking you some questions in a few minutes so we can get to know and trust each other.

"Who believes that hypnotism is real? Let's see a show of hands. Go on…there we go. Now, there's one thing you all need to know. Not everybody's able to be hypnotized. Did you know that? Yep, and I am a little hesitant to tell you this part, because it's not always well-received. Here's the deal: only intelligent and open-minded people can be hypnotized.

"How many of you are thinking it's getting a little toasty in here? A little sticky. Show of hands. Thank you. How many of y'all like grits? And I don't mean your instant kind of grits. I'm talking *real* grits—slow-cooking, bubbling-creamy grits. Butter and a lot of salt? Uh-huh, I see more hands now."

Mitch leaned forward slightly and saw that A.P., Shelby, and Lady A were all wide-eyed and locked in on Reverend Rooks.

Lady A looked over at Mitch, smiled, and whispered, "If I remember correctly, right about here's where he'll be askin' for some stage volunteers. Would you do it?" she asked.

While Mitch thought about an answer, Lady A started up again, and he never got his chance to respond.

"Well I wouldn't…no sirree…let somebody make a fool a me?" She elbowed Mitch lightly in the arm. "I do enough a that all by myself." She playfully nudged him again, this time in the ribs.

"Let's see now." Reverend Rooks sounded as if he was catching a second wind. "I'm looking out onto this vast and beautiful ocean of smart, willing, and esthetically pleasing volunteer candidates. So who's it going to be? Who's willing to help me out?"

Mitch saw several hands go up. Some popped up and then waved vigorously, and others rose slowly and incrementally.

"Let's see here…young man to my right…there you go. Come on up and stand right next to me," Reverend Rooks said, waving him forward.

Mitch saw that the volunteer was Ricky Hammond. Ricky jaunted toward the stage and broad jumped almost to the middle.

"Law have mercy," Shelby blurted. Laughter quickly followed from the two rows in front and in back of her. "Just double law have mercy," she repeated and set off more giggles.

Reverend Rooks seized Ricky's hand and swung him around like a slow-footed shag partner. "We got us a live one right here. I can just tell. May I have an encouraging amen? Thank you so much."

A.P. scooted up in his seat and waved frantically at Mitch. "This ain't gonna go well." A.P. got up and walked over to Mitch. "If they ask about imitating some kind a animal like they always do…" A.P. didn't finish the sentence. He returned to his seat.

Mitch pulled out a pen and tore off a corner of a program page. He began to write his response, but he realized with full certainty that A.P. was most likely talking about Ricky imitating the two-headed dog. He crumpled up the note and didn't pass it.

Reverend Rooks stood next to Ricky and scrutinized the other raised hands. "So, who else?" he asked. "Help me…okay, let's try a female. Even things out. You. Yes, you. Come on up here. We won't bite."

"Damn if he didn't say 'bite,'" Mitch thought. "Two-headed dog…and then 'bite'…this ain't shapin' up," he said, but not loud enough to be heard.

Mitch didn't recognize the young woman. A thin redhead, maybe college age. She approached the stage platform much less enthusiastically than Ricky. Reverend Rooks extended a hand and assisted her with the step up, and that touched off a rumble-hum that could have been a bad muffler on a distant highway. When Reverend Rooks walked her over to where Ricky stood, the vulnerability of her short skirt came into full view to the rest of the audience.

"My God, don't you see it?" Lady A squealed and grabbed Mitch's hand. It was loud enough to draw a look from Reverend Rooks. "You can't see it? It's right there in plain sight." She turned away from Mitch and picked up Shelby's hand and squeezed on her too.

Lady A's whispers and seat wiggles were drawing all kinds of looks. Mitch didn't know what to do or say, and the fragile factor of the first-date pressure paralyzed him. She shrieked one more time, and he couldn't hold back any longer. "It ain't *that* short…I've seen shorter." Mitch said and then turned to look into Lady A's eyes. They were balloons overstretched and about to detonate.

"No, no, no. Screw that." Lady A's words slid on loose gravel. "Look at that girl from the side…the way she pulls that red hair over…right there…ohhh…she could be Lori Leigh's twin sister. It's a sign…it's some kind a sign. I know a sign when I see it." Lady A extended her hands out in front of her toward the stage as if she were reaching for a platter of pot roast.

Mitch peered at the young female volunteer for a better look. He also wanted to please his date. After about a minute, he knew he wasn't seeing what Lady A was seeing. He looked over at Shelby and A.P., and they both had fixed looks toward the stage. They could have been stargazers trying to distinguish a planet from a star. He gave up waiting for their help.

"Now that we have our volunteers, let me ask them to answer me honestly and truthfully. Are you open minded? You can just shake your head. Thank you. Also, do you believe that you are capable and open minded enough to allow yourself to be hypnotized? Shake of the head for me? Thank you. Okay, let me start with our young man. Your name, friend?" Reverend Rooks asked in a whisper.

"Ricky Hammond, sir," he said and looked with a smile toward the audience.

"And what is your occupation, Ricky Hammond?"

"You mean what do I do to make money?"

"Yes, sir. Tell us a little bit of your work history." Reverend Rooks smiled at the audience, and that welled up a few laughs.

"Right now, I drive a tow truck. A wrecker. I took over my daddy's business, Hammond's Hookers," Ricky said and clapped along with the crowd, who applauded his business name. "And I used to work with that man, A.P. Thackston, sittin' right over there." Ricky waved at A.P. "Plumber's helper, you could call it."

"Thank you, Ricky, for *all* that," Reverend Rooks said and escorted Ricky over to the middle of the stage. "Ricky…have you ever felt thirsty?

I'm talking about the kind of thirsty where you were almost willing to drink anything just to stay alive."

"Oh, yes sir. Many times. You wanna know what for?" Ricky asked.

"No, let's hold on to that thirsty feeling for now. That's what I want you to remember and think about. How about music, Ricky? You do like music?" Rooks continued.

"Sure, yes sir."

"Good. Now, I want you to think real hard about a favorite song. Do you have an all-time absolute favorite?" Reverend Rooks walked slowly over to the podium and leaned on it heavily enough that its base screeched when it moved. He pulled out a handkerchief, wiped his forehead, and dabbed his swollen check.

Ricky watched the preacher and waited for him to look up again. "That's easy, Preacher Rooks. 'Sweet Home Alabama.' That's a Lynyrd Skynyrd song. They out a Jacksonville, Florida, where my cousins live. They're hippie chicks. And they know all them boys."

Mitch leaned toward Lady A. "Don'tcha think he's gettin' a little talky? Gettin' braver and braver. Pray he don't get asked about his favorite animal. A.P. says they always do that."

"That's fine, Ricky, real fine." Reverend Rooks walked back from the podium and looked at his volunteer. "Now, If I were to ask you to sing the first part of that song by...who was it? Leonard somebody? Could you do it?" Reverend Rooks stepped back.

"Yes sir, 'cept it's 'Lynyrd Skynyrd'. That's the way they say it."

"Promise me you will sing the first part of your favorite song. Just the first part. I'm sure you can do it. Look me in the eyes..." Reverend Rooks said and handed the mike over to Ricky.

"Uh-oh, there come the eyes thing," Ricky said and laughed once.

"Yes, concentrate on my eyes, Ricky, and think back on being thirsty like we talked about. Hold on to that mike, and you sing your favorite song. Sing what you need to sing." Reverend Rooks slowly eased away.

Ricky Hammond pressed the microphone against his chest and appeared to freeze after he closed his eyes.

"He's froze up," Mitch said. "Don't lock ya knees, Ricky…don't lock them knees."

Ricky opened his eyes, and his left arm shot out like a line-drive foul ball. He extended his right leg and tapped his foot. Then he started to bounce a little on his toes. Suddenly, his head flew back, and he belted out, "Turn it up…Big whee-uhls keep on turnin'. Carry me home to see my kin…"

The audience roared and rose to their feet. Many began to sing along with Ricky and clap in a perfect cadence. It got so loud they covered up Ricky's singing. Reverend Rooks moved in, placed his hand on the volunteer's forehead, and maintained that connection until Ricky stopped singing. He looked confused. The preacher caught the microphone just as it was about to slip out. Some in the crowd booed.

"Ladies and gentlemen…have we just discovered us a rock star or what?" declared Reverend Rooks.

The crowd rose and cheered again. Mitch, Lady A, Shelby, and A.P. slowly stood and clapped along with them.

"Damnedest thing I think I've ever seen," Mitch yelled while the ovation was starting to die down.

"Now, Ricky Hammond, Ricky the Rock Star, I'm going to ask you to do one more thing," Rooks said.

"Oh no, let that be it," A.P. said to Shelby. "No sir, let him go," he yelled toward the stage, but the surrounding crowd shushed him.

"We are going to take this to the next level, Ricky. You are knocking it out of the park."

"This shit ain't gon' flush, y'all," Mitch said. "Just please don't ask him to be any kind of animal," Mitch thought and closed his eyes.

"Since you are in the automotive trade, in a roundabout, end-of-the-road kinda way, I want you to think about all the cars you have ever towed. I'll give you a few seconds to think about that. Concentrate. Now, think about your favorite out of all those vehicles. So which one's your favorite?" Reverend Rooks said and waited on his volunteer.

"Surely," the preacher kept cajoling, "surely you have one in mind."

"Of all the things in the whole world…" Mitch said to Lady A.

"Yes sir, I do. I got one for ya." Ricky didn't skip a beat. "Sixty-five Pontiac...GTO...gold as your cufflinks, mags, whitewall tires..." Ricky rattled on and would have continued, but Reverend Rooks jumped in.

"Nailed it, Ricky. Now that we know your favorite car, here's the final thing." Rooks cleared his throat. "I think this will be the best way to wrap up the show. How about if I asked you to become that nineteen sixty-five gold Pontiac GTO? Could you do it? And what would you sound like?"

A.P. walked over to Mitch. "This ain't good, Mitch. This won't end well." A.P. sat in Mitch's seat and covered his eyes.

"He must be under some kind a spell," Mitch said.

Ricky lowered himself to the stage floor and rolled over onto his back. Then he sat up with his legs flat and stretched straight out. He extended his right arm and cupped his hand like he was holding onto something or someone. He pointed his left arm forward, and he was gripping what appeared to be an imaginary steering wheel. He steered over to the right, and then he pretended to back up. The crowd was mostly hushed, but some people laughed whenever he moved. In a few seconds, he began to cough. He eventually rolled over onto his right side and closed his eyes.

When Ricky stopped moving, Reverend Rooks got up from the stool, turned away from his star volunteer, and faced the audience. "Not sure what *that* GTO was doing for us right there, but hypnosis can transport us into unanticipated rooms and corridors of the mind. Ladies and gentleman, that's the first time in my twenty years of doing this show that we have ever had a volunteer imitate a car. Sometimes we can get someone to do a song or persuade somebody to be a chicken or a cow, but never an automobile. So please give our volunteer, Ricky Hammond, your warmest ovation."

"Everybody's got to know whose car that was," Mitch said.

"The way that crowd acted, maybe the hell not," A.P. said.

Once the applause for Ricky came to an end, Ricky climbed to his feet, walked quickly off the stage, and headed for the men's restroom, which set off a trill of giggling from the part of the crowd who could see him.

"Well, forgive our volunteer. He was up here a lonnng time," Rooks said.

In a few seconds, Ricky emerged from the restroom holding a toilet plunger in his right hand. He returned to the stage, stopped, and lifted up the plunger as if it were a torch. He held out his other arm, pushed one leg forward, and then locked himself into a stance as if he were a statue. The audience buzzed. No one could tell if that was the hypnosis or Ricky.

"Dear audience, that's all the gas I've got in my tank, but it's been fun. Please, let's hear it for my manager, Knox Gallman. He held things together while I was running late. And even though we didn't get to hear from her, how about a hand for our other volunteer." Rooks swept his hand around toward where the young lady had been standing, but she was gone. "She has apparently stepped away. Please thank her for me when you see her in town. I hope you enjoyed the sermon and the show. We are coming to that crass business part of our show, and I do apologize, but we've got to keep the lights on. If you feel so indicated by the nudge from above, we do accept love offerings, and please visit my book table set up near the exit. I've also got some photos. I'll gladly sign any of that for you. Let's end with prayer, shall we?"

"I'm just shocked," Mitch said as the four of them walked out in the middle of Rooks's closing prayer.

"A.P., let's go back and check on Ricky," Shelby finally said. "He didn't look right, not at all. Come on with me, A.P. Y'all head on back to the restaurant. Enjoy y'all's first date. We'll be there after while. I'm worried about Ricky. That boy's always been so fragile. Oh, Mitch, I talked to Sharona Riddle. Ask me later."

CHAPTER 36

Mitch and Lady A pressed against each other arm to arm, and they picked up speed and bull-rushed to make it through the crowd and the narrow exit doors of the furniture warehouse. Once they were outside, Mitch felt the breeze chilling the sweat on his cheeks. He was surprised when she squeezed him around the bicep with both hands and didn't let go.

Clumps of dispersing spectators were drifting off, and some of them stopped and circled up. They could have been musicians warming up their instruments and filling the air with their mishmash of squeals and buzz talk. Mitch and Lady A weaved through them and sometimes got forced from the sidewalk onto the softer lawn grass. They raised their voices as they tried their best to catch up on everything that had just occurred.

"You mean to tell me," Lady A howled, "Rooks got whacked on the head, *and* it was one a them deacons?"

"And that man lying in the bushes, he was all out a sorts." Mitch said. "And when I seen him come limpin' across that stage…"

"Maybe it's my hunger talkin', but I got mixed feelings about the whole thing," Lady A said.

"No way in hell Ricky Hammond should a been volunteerin'." Mitch was trying his best to jump in to agree with her.

"Noooo, I mean…was Ricky fakin'?" she asked. "I mean, the way he just folded up his tent when Rooks asked him to *be* a car. And then he chose *that* car…near and dear. Seems rigged, in a way."

"Of all the people in Fountainville...Ricky Hammond. It would have to be a pretty big-ass spell, is what I'm sayin'," Mitch said. "And I admit, when I walked in here tonight, hypnotism was total BS, through and through. But what we just saw...makes me think."

"I was just the opposite," she said. "Goin' in, I was a big believer."

"How 'bout now?" Mitch asked.

"Flotsam and jetsam. Nothin' more, nothin' less," she said and squeezed his arm a little tighter.

Mitch didn't know what she meant, but it didn't matter at all. "Still good for coffee and dessert?" he asked, hoping it was still on.

They crossed Main Street in perfect tandem and headed for Sweet Shelby's. As soon as the door shut behind them, Mitch looked for the weather vane and the north and south board. It simply read SHIFTING WINDS.

He got Lady A to take a look, and she squinted without saying anything. "Look at her green eyes," he thought.

A waitress led them to a booth, and they ordered two coffees and one peach cobbler to share. Once the waitress left them, Lady A kept her menu and playfully tapped it on top of his hand. Out of nowhere, she asked him in a low whisper, "You got a girl back in Columbia, Mitch Beam?"

The menu taps followed by the question knocked the thinking breath right out of him for a moment. "Trollin' cases don't give me much time for romance, you know..."

"Well, my sister's gettin' you plenty a cases...and...here *we* are," Lady A said and smiled. "In fact, Kathy wanted me to tell you she's got another good one for ya."

He felt his response clogging up in bumper-to-bumper traffic. "Kathy's a lifesaver," he said.

"Seems like you keep that Cutlass burnin' up the road. Comin' and goin'. Comin' and goin'," she said.

"I come into this world, and I'll be a goin' out too. It's a pattern, tried and true. Key's doin' something in all the meantimes." Mitch wasn't sure where that came from.

"I tell you what I think. That is...if you wanna know," she said.

"Oh yeah. Yeah, definitely," he said.

"Trollin' cases for a TV show, that's fine and all. But it looks to me like it ain't nothin' but the Mitch Beam way a wanderin'. That's…all…it…is—wanderin'," Lady A said.

To Mitch, it looked as if she had more to say, but the waitress materialized without making a sound and handed them their coffees and cobbler. He wasted no time doctoring up his coffee, clanking his spoon several times.

"I'm just thinkin'." Lady A stopped to spoon some cobbler. "My dear Lori Leigh…she used to say all the time, whenever she was talkin' about Myron, 'All Myron wants to do is get out on that golf tour.' And then she'd say, 'A wise traveler knows when it's time to rest.'" Lady A sighed. "And by the way, I don't know what came over me back there, saying that redheaded volunteer girl looked like Lori Leigh. I guess I was just hoping."

"I hear ya." Mitch waited before jumping in too soon. "So let's talk about you. Since you're poundin' me like hard dough. How come you've never gotten married? I mean, as pretty as you are?"

Lady A laughed and took another bite of cobbler. "I guess I'm just a handful, Mitch Beam." The waitress walked by with fresh coffee, and Lady A lifted her cup. "Some people tell me, I'm always gonna be married to my dress shop."

"I can see that," he said. "I mean, with that bra-couch and all…"

They laughed and talked about more things, including his first visit to the shop, and they drank more coffee and nibbled cobbler crust for about an hour until the waitress returned to their table. "I've got a message from Miss Shelby. She told me to pass along that she and A.P. won't be joining y'all. She didn't want to intrude on y'all's date. And Mr. Mitch, she said she needs your help cleanin' out Mr. Billy's place. And she said for you to meet her there tomorrow morning. Around ten. Then she said, real serious like. 'Be on time, please.' Now, no rush. We 'bout to close, but stay long as you like. We'll be cleaning up, so ignore us. Oh, and Miss Shelby said y'all's pie and coffee are on the house…so no check."

The waitress slipped away into the kitchen, and Lady A spoke up. "That's gonna be some killer day you got in front of ya."

"It's gonna be tougher on her. Shelby's not always as strong as she lets on," Mitch said and slid the plate over with the last bite of peach cobbler. "Peach for a peach." He couldn't believe he came up with that one and that he said it out loud.

"What a fine gentleman. Tell me now, 'Mr. Mitch'…I love the way she called you that. I been wantin' to ask you this ever since you popped up out a nowhere, after all these years. Askin' all kinds a questions. Why in the world do you want to know all this about Myron and Lori Leigh, and also all those cases my sister's been diggin' up for ya?" Lady A asked and sat back.

"It's hard to put in words. Bout the only thing I can think of is…I just like it," he said and grabbed his coffee cup and looked into it for several seconds before he took a swig. "Ugh…went ice cold on me."

"You just gotta know stuff, right? You love knowledge, don't ya?" Lady A asked. Mitch watched as she leaned across the table. "Let me tell you this, Mr. Mitch. Straight up. Knowledge never loves back."

He escorted her to the parking lot, and they lingered at her car door for a few minutes. He didn't know what to do next except to rehash fragments of their earlier conversation. Lady A sprang forward and surprised him with a kiss. She planted it right in the middle of a sentence. His hand slid off the door handle twice, but somehow the door flumped open. Her tires crackled backing up, and he watched her long after her tail lights topped over a hill crest.

On the way back to A.P.'s, Scuffletown was moonless and still. He thought about Lady A's questions as he drove past the remains of the Stairley plantation house as well as Gilreath Farms. When he was directly across from the burned-out dance barn, he spotted a line of peacocks that appeared to be hell bent on crossing the road. He slowed and skidded to a stop just a few feet away from the terrified birds. They planted themselves in the middle and wouldn't move. He tapped his horn a few times, but they only slow danced in small circles. While he waited, a luna moth dropped out of nowhere. Enormous lime-green wings adorned with eyelike spots. It began to play in and out of the high beams and then looped up and over the windshield, landing gracefully on the wiper blade. It folded and unfolded its wings several times, leaped upward, hovered for a moment, and then ascended into the stars.

CHAPTER 37

The following morning, Mitch woke up before sunrise. For the span of three coffee refills, he rocked alone on A.P.'s front porch trying to paint a coat of meaning on the night before. Ground fog obscured the first sight of the sun, which seemed to struggle to do a pull-up over the uneven tops of loblollies.

He studied a tulip poplar along the edge of the front drive just as it let go of two or three of its golden leaves. They twirled and glimmered and settled briefly onto the grass until another gust tumbled them farther on into a swale. Fallen sweet-gum balls could be seen already gathered along the sides of the driveway even though the only sweet-gum trees were across the road. He listened to a sweet-gum ball captured by a leaf drum-brushing across the porch.

"So…" A.P.'s voice behind him was like a rifle shot. "Man, I saw you jump. Sorry. So, how'd it go?"

"Hypnotist…horrible. Date…great," Mitch said and stopped rocking.

"Yeah, we thought y'all had those goo-goo eyes goin' at each other. We didn't wanna bust in on it," A.P. said. "Really, Shelby said not to."

"Smart woman. And one you don't deserve, boss man." Mitch got up and playfully bumped A.P.'s chair with his hip. "Want coffee?"

"Yeah, give it to me black," A.P. said. "Had me two bowls a her banana puddin'. I still got the sugar shakes."

When Mitch returned with the coffee, he asked about Ricky.

"Well, you know…Ricky's always been a little…you know, tetched. All them drugs he and Billy did…" A.P. closed his eyes and went into a gentle rock. "A little nippy out here."

"Feels kinda good," Mitch said. "Helps me think."

"You got our message, didn't ya?" A.P. asked. "Cleanin' out that shed? Shelby and Ricky worked it all out between the two of 'em. I really didn't wanna be a part a talkin' 'bout that hypnotist. I was too pissed. So I just went outside while she checked on him. They set up the whole shed-cleaning deal. And Shelby said, 'He's fine. He's just being Ricky.'"

"Yep. Been sittin' here thinkin' about that too," Mitch said.

"No tellin' what you 'bout to find in that shed," A.P. said and sipped his coffee. "When Billy went up there to live for good, Shelby never would go inside that thing. Hospital brought him back down to Shelby's to die. And that's what he did, mercifully. Two days later. That's when I called you."

"I'm guessin' I can do it all myself, if Shelby wants. Just gimme the word," Mitch said. "It might be best."

"Naw," A.P. said and stopped. "She needs to do it. Help put it behind her. But here's what I do wantcha to do. Get up to Ricky's about an hour early. That way, if there's bad stuff lyin' around inside that shed, you go ahead and trash it before she sees it. And one more thing: my back's out a whack. I won't be comin' with you."

"Yeah, that's a plan," Mitch said and looked at his watch. "I best get truckin'."

"Clearing out the earthly trappings of Billy Cole…that ain't exactly what I call a dream weekend," A.P. said. "Thank ya, man. Oh, I got a message on the phone. Berry Gilreath—he just said something about his closing got done, and please call him when you can."

"Sounds like I got me a helluva case this time. I owe both you *and* Shelby. Takin' care a me while I found me some cases. And settin' me up last night." Mitch smiled and went inside to get dressed.

CHAPTER 38

Mitch's Cutlass rolled out of A.P.'s drive that morning at a quarter till nine. As he drove away, A.P. stood and raised his coffee mug as if he were blessing the launch of a top-secret military operation. The old Hammond junkyard had its fortress on the opposite end of town on Glenn Garrett Road, a dirt trail mostly that dead-ended near a cliff beside Grigsby Swamp. According to local legend, the Hammond family, over the course of a century or more, had dumped moonshine stills, weapons, dead gamecocks, and even a few ballot boxes into their snake-infested bogland.

When he was close enough to read the billboard for Hammond's Hookers, he slid to a stop, and the bank of sand at the bottom of their drive flew up and tap danced lightly across his windshield and roof. He looked hard for some sign of activity. Next to a padlocked shed, two rollbacks were parked on humped rows of clay where a small garden had probably thrived at one time. Off to the side, a toppled Michelin Man scarecrow lay underneath an old retread.

The larger truck had mud flaps with silhouettes of naked ladies. A raggedy MIA-POW flag stretched across the smaller truck's cab window. Two identical stickers barely held on to each bumper: IF YOU DON'T LIKE MY DRIVING—PLEASE CALL 1-800-EAT-SHIT.

Mitch slowly made his way up Ricky's mobile home steps. Before he reached the landing, he looked toward the junkyard. From that perspective, he could see, at least partially, over the top of the junkyard screen. "Always wondered what the hell was back there," he thought. Car hulks and car-part scrapheaps made up the rows of an automobile graveyard that ran all the way into an adjoining pasture.

There were voices coming from inside, and they appeared to be competing with a blender and "Free Bird." Mitch didn't have any trouble recognizing the distinct smell of the smoke. He was glad he had listened to A.P. about coming early.

He knocked, and then it sounded like a poorly thrown bowling ball. The music disappeared. He heard one more stumble, and then someone approached the door, singing way out of kilter. "I'm Ricky the Hook, the wrecker of woe and the wiper of slates." The door flished open, and Ricky Hammond stared at his visitor. He finally spoke. "What can I do you for? Oh, hay-ell. I thought y'all was comin' at ten. Let me clean up." He slung the door, but it only made it halfway into the door frame.

Mitch never got the chance to speak. He turned and stepped across the front porch and stood on his tiptoes to see over the fence for potential places to dump Billy's stuff.

The door pulled open again. Out wobbled Ricky Hammond. He wore an Alice Cooper T-shirt and jeans with knee patches. "Y'all here *way* early. I'm good on time. I looked." The cold air didn't seem to bother him at all.

"Where'd your friends go?" Mitch asked.

"Don't worry…they're gone. Where's Miss Shelby?" Ricky asked. He flipped a cigarette and caught it in his lips, and he offered his pack to Mitch.

"She's comin' later on. Maybe best for me to take a look inside that shed first," Mitch said. He was a little fidgety about getting started, so he moved toward the steps to coax Ricky into action.

"I love Miss Shelby. That right there's a good woman. Paid Billy's rent, sent us food." Ricky coughed, and it sounded like walking through a leaf pile. "We talked after the show," Ricky said.

"Since you mentioned last night…" Mitch started.

"Shelby done asked me all that could be asked about that show last night." Ricky took a drag off his cigarette. "I'll tell you the very same thing I told her…I don't remember nothin'."

"Nothin'?" Mitch asked. "Not one single thing?"

"Not a damn thing, except I remember holdin' a plunger right there at the end. And then everybody was clappin' and carryin' on."

"But you volunteered…why?" Mitch asked.

"Shelby's done beat you to the punch on that one. All I know's people said I did a good job."

"But what made you do it?" Mitch asked.

"That man got to askin' all kinds a questions. And just like that, something snapped, and I did it. That's all I know. Oh, yeah, and the plunger." Ricky laughed. "Both Shelby and A.P. told me after the show I looked like warmed-up shit. Which I told them I took exception to. I was a little tired, but that's all."

"You ready?" Mitch asked and stepped toward the shed. "I hope you got a key."

"A key?" Ricky slung around a key chain that could have been mistaken for a string of crappie. He had at least a hundred keys of all colors and sizes. "I'll find it on here somewhere."

They walked about twenty yards to get to the shed. It appeared to be mostly sheet metal. One door, no windows, and an air-conditioning unit that balanced in an opening somehow, thanks to a couple of two-by-fours and gobs of caulk.

"It ain't so bad," Ricky told Mitch as he continued to try his keys. "Billy liked it fine."

"This thing got any power hooked up?" Mitch asked.

"Oh hayell yeah. Woodstove, refrigerator, new shower head too," Ricky said.

"How long he stay here?" Mitch asked.

"About five years, right up to his cancer. And that's when he went back to Miss Shelby," Ricky said and continued to look for the right key. "I'll be right back."

Ricky walked over behind the rollbacks and disappeared. Mitch took a knee trying to imagine how Billy could have lived in such a confined space. He looked at the padlock again and saw for the first time, in another angle of light, the faded shape on the door where a cross must have been hung.

"He asked me to let him paint that door red." Ricky's voice made Mitch jump. "Never said why. I didn't have a problem with it."

"Find a key?" Mitch asked.

"Well yeah, in a way." Ricky lifted up a pair of bolt cutters. "Now watch this."

Ricky swung the bolt cutters up to chest level. He let out a yelp and rushed the red door. From a distance he could have been mistaken for a sleep- and food-impoverished commander leading a desperate rebel assault.

Mitch lagged behind on purpose and marveled at the way Ricky worked on crunching that padlock at different angles. In the midst of Ricky clacking and air gulping, he began to think about many of the events that had come before this moment of entering Billy's sanctuary.

Fountainville was proving to be a fertile source for trolling cases, and his extended homecoming had easily yielded him his first long-awaited trolling wins, including a possible relationship with a childhood crush.

All the traveling and stops along Scuffletown Road seemed more and more like troubled sea expeditions to sail around the Cape of Good Hope. As he found himself on the verge of following Ricky through the open shed door, he had a curiosity that was heartbreaking and hopeful all at once.

CHAPTER 39

"There's a drop cord in here somewhere," Ricky said as he vanished into the blackness of Billy's shed. In a few seconds, the bolt cutters scraped something and ka-lunked to the floor.

Mitch stayed put. He tried his best to see inside but saw nothing.

"I will say this much," Ricky said. "It might behoove me to take off these damn shades."

Mitch was beginning to feel useless and growing antsy thinking Shelby might get a view of Billy's contents before he would. "Somebody told me way back," he said, and waited to see if Ricky was paying any attention.

"I'm listenin'," Ricky's voice sputtered as if obstructed by something large inside.

"They were trying to explain what darkness really is. First, they said it's nothing to be scared of. Then they said it's just some light that's never been told a good story." Mitch waited for a response.

"You know what?" Ricky asked in a half holler. "Maybe that's the reefer doin' the listenin', but that makes perfect damn sense to me. A good story, if you tell it just right, can do some good shit. And…looky here. Let me pull this line over this rafter. And let's see if we got a bulb. Yep, we got light. Come on in."

Gingerly, Mitch eased through the doorway. He passed by a long table that ran the length of the building. It was covered with hundreds of tent caterpillars, some moving, some not, and one wall panel was embellished by several dozen butterflies and moths, pinned and labeled. Cocoons and chrysalis remnants were strewn all over the desk and floor.

The drop cord that Ricky had somehow found and thrown over the central beam plumb-bobbed above them. After a few minutes, it eventually settled into a true stopping point. "I'm glad that thing stopped swingin'," Mitch said. "It was making me seasick."

"You see all that butterfly and moth shit?" Ricky asked Mitch. "Billy got all into it. Especially after he got the verdict on his radiation result."

"What's a can a spray paint doin' right there in the middle of the floor?" Mitch asked. "It sort a sticks out. Looks like it's got a note to it." Mitch got to the note first and read it. "Just says, 'For Ricky. Thanks.'"

Ricky didn't comment. He stepped over to the shed door and closed it. "Just before Billy died, he said he had something in here for me. I didn't have the gonads to come up here for it. Not by myself. And...promise me. On what I'm about to say. Promise me you won't do something crazy, like go to Swanger or let on any of it to Miss Shelby?"

"Lemme hear it," Mitch said.

"You know how Swanger always blamed any—and I mean *any*—kind a vandalism on Myron? Even spray-paintin' signs?" Ricky asked. "Well..."

"Well what?" Mitch asked.

"We were the ones. Me and Billy. The whole time." Ricky laughed, and it seemed to break something loose deep in his lungs and grew into a coughing spell.

"Swanger still believes it was Myron. That's what he told me," Mitch said. "He said his proof was how all the sign paintin' came to an end just as soon as Myron was gone."

"We really just stopped wantin' to do it. That's all," Ricky said. "There's something more to it." Ricky left Mitch hanging.

"And, yeah, now that you mention it," Mitch said, "I remember seeing one a them signs. Funny as hell. And didn't it have something to do with Swanger?" Mitch asked.

"Our first one was all about Swanger," Ricky said. "We sprayed 'SWANGER' under 'STOP.' Then the word we got was how our sign pushed Swanger's button. So when we heard that, that's the thing that made us keep on doin' it."

"How many signs?" Mitch asked.

"Chamber of commerce sign, south end of town. We changed 'WELCOME TO FOUNTAINVILLE'. It ended up sayin' 'DON'T COME TO SWANGERVILLE.'" Ricky laughed again and abruptly stopped. "There was a bunch of 'em we did."

"Swanger ever do anything about it?" Mitch asked.

"After he pitched a fit, he'd go straight to Myron. Aggravate him about it. Then the trusty prisoners got trucked out there to do some sign cleanin'. Swanger called it 'community service,'" Ricky said. "There's something more to it."

"So what else got painted?" Mitch asked.

"You can't tell this to nobody. I mean nobody," Ricky said.

"Go on with it." Mitch waited for Ricky to continue. In that space of silence, the door squeaked on its hinges, and both men jumped. False alarm.

"That night...and I'm talkin' about *that* night..." Ricky began and stopped. "We just finished sprayin' up Swanger's brand-new speed limit sign. The one leadin' down Scuffletown near Gilder Creek. We changed 'SPEED LIMIT 45' to 'PEE VOMIT,' then we wiped out the '45' and painted 'SWANGER.'"

"That same night?" Mitch asked. "Y'all see anything? Who knows any of this?"

"Two now, countin' you," Ricky said. "Maybe three, 'cause we thought we saw Berry Gilreath walkin' around that night. Can't swear to it, though."

"Anything more?" Mitch asked.

"Nothin' about this can ever go to Miss Shelby. You gotta swear. It's part a my pledge to Billy," Ricky said.

"Go ahead." Mitch closed his eyes and waited for the next shoe to drop.

"We were cleanin' up and just about to leave. We heard a car comin'. We just knew it was Swanger, so we dropped and hid. But it ended up bein' Myron and Lori Leigh. Myron passed us, stopped, turned off his headlights, and backed into this gap up near the Gilreath Farm gate. We finished cleanin' up our tracks, anything that might lead to us."

"Is that when y'all left?" Mitch asked.

"Right before we took off on foot, Billy said somethin' like, 'If Swanger goes on patrol, even he'll see our sign. And then he'll see Myron's car. I gotta warn 'em.'"

"Shit fire, Ricky," Mitch said.

"So Billy took off to run down there, but he stopped and spun around and came back. He said, 'I can't do it. Myron'll think I'm spyin', and Swanger's too blind to see 'em anyway. Let's go.' So that's what we did. We took off, and when we got farther up near the Five Forks, I went my way home, and he went his way."

Mitch held his hands above his head. "I don't know what to say."

"He swore me to never tell. But with him gone, I gotta let it out to somebody. And then, that next morning, when we found out…it's been pure tee hell ever since. And it ate Billy up, slap up. Ate him up to death, if you ask me."

"All these years, Ricky…all these years," Mitch said.

"And you see what happens in this town if you get caught in the blame game? We sure as hell would a been in the mix too. I gotta say, though, the hell of blamin' ourselves…that was punishment enough. That's the way we came to see it.

"But, Mitch, here's one good thing. Shelby *does* need to know this. It might give her some peace a mind. Hold on to that table a caterpillars right there, 'cause this might be some sweet icing on the cake for her: Billy upped and got hisself saved. She might not even know. You'd think word might a made its way round this whole town, in the usual way gossip does. But I don't know." Ricky smiled. "And me too…bigger than hell. Right before he got too sick to get out. He had me drive him down to that interdenominational church. The one on this side a the interstate. Preacher McConnell, I think he said his name was. He told us what we needed to do. And we prayed to get it all wiped away. And we both said, almost at the same time, that sounded too good to be true. But the preacher promised it was true, and damn if we didn't get dunked right in front a that whole church. And they backed it up with certificates. The whole works."

Mitch was doing all he could to stifle crying right in Ricky's face. "She does need to know that. Would be a real blessing. Sure would," Mitch said.

"Then, on the way back from gettin' dunked—you'll appreciate this—Billy told me, 'Throwin' in the towel to Jesus was the best loss I ever won.' And that's word for word. He really got into his butterflies then. Had me climbing into that crabapple tree collecting caterpillars for him. He found his peace, but then, damn if the big C didn't take care a that."

They stood there in silence for a good five minutes. Occasionally the two of them looked up at each other as if they had discovered Amelia Earhart's missing Lockheed Model 10-E Electra and couldn't figure out what to do about it.

"That's a lot to take in, but Shelby's about to get here. Billy ain't got much a nothin' in here, does he? And on big stuff. Is this all he had?" Mitch asked.

"He did tell me the last time he left this place. He said if Mitch Beam was to ever come back to town, he had somethin' for you too. That's likely to be it right over there. Over on top of his bed quilt. He said you'd know what it was."

The two of them eased over to the bed. A red shirt was folded neatly, and an aluminum dipper was laid on top. Mitch held the jersey up. 'Tex-ize' was printed across the front. He clutched the dipper to his chest. Mitch couldn't talk. His eyes filled, and they could have been a pair of culverts carrying a swollen stream under a roadway. "Never thought I'd…"

There was a light tap on the door, and in walked Shelby Shillinglaw with something of a blank expression. She was holding a box of Krispy Kremes as if it were a football. "Well, you rascal. You *did* get here on time," she said to Mitch. "And how's our hypnotist hero?" She gave Ricky a light punch on his arm.

"Not so much stuff in here," she said, "so thank the Lord on that, 'cause I ain't in the mood to handle it. I'm receiving it as a blessing. Here, y'all have at them doughnuts. I'm watchin' my weight." She handed the doughnut box to Ricky, put her hands on her hips, and looked at the caterpillars blanketing the whole side of the shed. Mitch didn't know what she might be thinking. He thought about the weather vane and what weather forecast he would like to chalk in at the very moment.

"I can load every bit a this stuff, Miss Shelby," Mitch said. "Take me up to five minutes. Tops. Ricky, why don't you walk her outside and tell her that Billy story you just then told me. The one about what happened to you and Billy at the church right off the interstate."

"Be my honor," Ricky said. "Miss Shelby?" He extended his arm for her. She didn't disagree, not even once, and Ricky, like any good shepherd, escorted the dispirited lamb to sit on his front porch.

Mitch gazed at Shelby's face as Ricky held her hand and spoke gently to her. In a few seconds she turned and looked upward with the kind of expression of fulfillment he had only seen in religious paintings of angels.

CHAPTER 40

After Shelby departed, Mitch and Ricky made a team business decision to save Billy's Bible and what looked like a prayer journal for Miss Shelby. They stuffed the rest of Billy's stuff into a couple of large boxes and then pushed them into the back seat of a stripped Barracuda. "For some reason, Billy liked him a Barracuda," Ricky told Mitch. "Don't ask me how I can remember shit like that."

"I'm a Cutlass man, myself. Love that rocket V-8. Gives me that power punch. Satisfies me somehow," Mitch said. "Now, what about you? If you was choosin' a vehicle, I just wonder what would it be?" he asked Ricky and laughed.

Ricky didn't speak for a minute or so. "This might surprise ya."

"I doubt it. I really do," Mitch said too low to be heard. He waited for Ricky to spill his guts, finally, about all that hypnosis silliness.

"I wouldn't even go for a car. They don't do one damn thing for me. I'll take a pickup any ol' time." Ricky stopped. "And most likely...a Chevy."

Mitch just stared at Ricky as if he had just streaked buck naked on Easter Sunday down the main aisle of the Fountainville First Baptist sanctuary. He couldn't think of any right words that wouldn't hurt Ricky to the core of his soul.

"Here, take this ten dollars and scrape up them caterpillars," Mitch said. "And just put 'em down at the base a that crabapple tree, and let 'em just run wild. We good here?"

"Yeah. We're good."

CHAPTER 41

Mitch was relieved to be done with Billy's shed. It also pleased him to remove that huge weight from Miss Shelby's shoulders. Billy's gifts to him were priceless. On the ride back, he tried to imagine all the hours, days, and years that Billy and Ricky suppressed their secrets, and also all they did to themselves as they wrestled their demons.

Their story was safe with him, but he wondered if he should have given Ricky greater assurance about that. They had suffered enough.

He felt a palpable nudge not to take the shorter route back to Scuffletown and A.P.'s place, so he stayed straight and headed toward Main Street instead.

As he neared the town limits and Fonda's Muffler Shop, there was a sprawling commotion ahead. An eighteen-wheeler trailer had turned over on its side, with its load of steel pipes sprawled and blocking every lane. When he came to a stop on the shoulder, many stranded drivers were already standing outside their vehicles.

In a few minutes, Chief Swanger's patrol car, with blue lights swirling, approached the overturned cab at just above earthworm speed. Swanger got out and walked over to one of the larger pipes. He attempted to shift it with his foot, but the pipe didn't budge an inch. He went back to his vehicle and reached in for his radio. A small crowd gathered around him. He motioned them to back up. In a while there were more sirens.

Since everything was mud-stuck, Mitch got another nudge to walk about fifty yards over to Fonda's Muffler Shop. He joined a family that had just arrived in a Volkswagen van. California tags. They all spilled out and took turns reading the bronze plaque for the Mighty Co and then to stare up at the statue.

A man with a Polaroid camera moseyed up, talked to the man and woman, and then arranged them and their five children for a picture in front of the statue. Mitch leaned in a little closer so he could also read the plaque. He tried to remember why he had never stopped to visit there.

"Wanna picture?" The man walked up from behind him, and Mitch never heard him. "Only five bucks," the man said.

Mitch stared at the man's pony tail. The way it fanned at the back reminded him of one of Billy's mounted moths.

"You must be Mr. Fonda?" Mitch asked.

"The one and only...and I know you too. Bob and Debra Dale Beam. You're their boy?"

"Good memory, sir," Mitch said.

"Yes, they're good people. Good customers. Moved to Greenville, right?" Fonda asked.

"Got backed up in all that over there. Just glad I wasn't in it," Mitch said and turned to check the status of the cleanup. "Thought I'd finally make myself take a look at your muffler man. Always told myself I would. Just never did it for some reason."

"Mighty glad you did. Take all the time ya need," Fonda said. Then he nimbly shifted over toward another couple. "Let me know if you folks wantcha picture made. Make a fine conversation piece."

Mitch soon became aware that Fonda had drifted back his way, and he felt compelled to say something.

"Can't tell ya the number of times I've driven by this thing," Mitch said. "No offense; it just kind a spooked me."

"Well whatcha think now, now that you've seen it up close?" Fonda asked.

"So where does a person come by getting something like that?" Mitch asked and walked up and placed his hand on what looked like a patch across the muffler man's torso. "Are these real parts?"

"Oh, they're real all right. Go ahead and touch it," Fonda said and then took a couple of steps toward the other couple again. In a few seconds, he reappeared to Mitch. "You asked where it came from…hell, I can't remember shit like that. Now…if you was to ask me who won the World Series, or the Carolina/Clemson game, that's the only kind a spaghetti sticks in my brain nowadays."

"Oh, it's comin' back to me now," Mitch said. "I see it when I look all the way up there. I always thought the muffler man looked like he was flipping his middle finger at somebody, maybe the whole world. I gotta be honest. See that part up there?"

"Huh…you see all that?" Fonda asked. "Never even thought about it." Fonda moved away from Mitch for good and set up the couple for their souvenir photo.

By the time Mitch walked back to his car, one lane had already opened up, and traffic was moving again. He was glad but also a little troubled over his first encounter with the muffler man.

CHAPTER 42

Over the next week, Mitch assisted Lady A in getting her shop all gussied up for the upcoming Winter Line Season Pleazins. He laughed at himself one day when he realized he had spent an hour and a half laying out a whole endcap of bras and girdles.

He delivered Billy's books to Miss Shelby, and, at her insistence, he left a pot of Shasta daisies at the Pink House along with a note for Miss Sharona.

On another day, he picked up the signed contract from Berry Gilreath, who bear-hugged him and wrinkled the contract. "You best be glad Miss Kathy Moss didn't see that," he thought. A short time later, he pumped gas at the pump next to Bud Culdock at Henderson's Stop-N-Go, and he tried, unsuccessfully, to engage Culdock with a question about whether the Cubs would ever win the World Series.

—

On Friday morning of that week, he heard A.P. knocking and moving around real early, as if he might be packing. "Where ya headed?" Mitch asked.

"Charlotte...again," A.P. said. "Ain't no easy way to get there from here. But good thing is, I might have another bank job lined up. They must a liked what I did on that last one. You?"

"I'm driving this Gilreath-Reames contract down to Atlanta. Do a little song and dance. If they like it, then I'll be takin' you and Miss Shelby out…well, and Lady A too. Cash starts burnin' a hole just as soon as it hits my pocket."

"You sure been putting some miles on that Cutlass," A.P. said. "Prob'ly good for thinkin', I guess."

"Mostly, I'd say for remember-thinkin'."

"So you and Lady A, huh? How about that," A.P. said.

"Yeah, yeah. I guess so. Like she says, she's a handful."

"We ain't talked about this for a while, but believe it or not, people think 'cause you're livin' here, I got the inside scoop on any kind a Myron-and-Lori Leigh story. That gonna happen?" A.P. asked. "People hopin' for a movie, TV special, or something good to come out of it. You know how people wish and talk, wish and talk."

"You know what?" Mitch started and then thought more about how he wanted to finish his sentence. "Something might. We'll see. I ain't ruled it in, and I ain't ruled it out. Sometimes, though, you just gotta leave some fish in the pond. Amen?"

"I hear ya. Now getcha ass down there. Bring us some a that Hot-Lanta moolah," A.P. said and toted his bag to his pickup. "Tomorrow, man."

On the way out of town, Mitch sensed a combination of heaviness and hope about Fountainville. He swung by Lady A's, and she handed him a Tupperware bowl full of chocolate-chip cookies. From there he drove through Scuffletown for just a small stretch before he turned off early onto Patton Pond Road to head to the interstate. He glanced at the bucket seat to his right, double-checking to make sure he had the contract. He had a good feeling about the new Gilreath-Reames case. Once he left the ramp to join the highway traffic, he never even thought about needing the radio.

At that instant, the highway seemed to burst wide open like Billy Cole's padlocked shed, receiving and then illuminated by a flood of new light. In the rhythm of the wheels underneath, he could almost hear a horse galloping out of control. Soon, that settled into a rattling backstop and the distant pops of baseballs and gloves. Screams of "Tex-ize stinks… Tex-ize stinks." A plunked batting helmet. Fuzzy thoughts. And then the redeeming voice of an angel announcing, "That ain't nothing but spilt water." And then he could feel and hear fists pounding, tires yawing, and fires crack-snapping on Scuffletown Road. For him it continued to bend and crest and descend into branch bowers and kudzu thickets, over unseen river water, and then to emerge from darkness and into speckled and brilliant light, but never completely to straighten.

ABOUT THE AUTHOR

Tommy Cofield is a poet, short-story writer, and novelist. He grew up in the upstate of South Carolina, and he learned to drive a stick shift on Scuffletown Road. He is a practicing attorney in Lexington, South Carolina. He attended the University of South Carolina, where he studied creative writing under James Dickey and William Price Fox. He and his wife, Janet, live in Lexington, South Carolina, and they have two adult children, T.J. Cofield and Caitlin Carolina Cofield. *Scuffletown* is his first novel.

ACKNOWLEDGMENTS

I deeply appreciate the editing advice, wisdom, and encouragement graciously provided by Signe Pike, who writes so elegantly.

I also acknowledge the wonderful teachers I have had along the way, including, but not limited to, my fourth-grade teacher, Elaine Hudson, who read *Charlotte's Web* and *Stuart Little* so inspiringly; my English teachers in high school, including Mollie Richardson, Thelma Wright, and Helen Sloan; and my University of South Carolina professors, Jack Ashley, who once opened a course on Southern literature by reciting, word for word, "A Good Man Is Hard to Find"; Kevin Lewis, for his encouragement; William Price Fox, for providing me opportunities to talk "writing" with the likes of Kurt Vonnegut, Tom Wolfe, John Gardner, Richard Wilbur, and others; and James Dickey, who could really tell a story and read and quote poetry like no other.

I also acknowledge my encouragers who pushed me toward and over the finish line, especially my daughter, Caitlin. Gratitude also to Mickey Mauldin, Aida Rogers, Terry Parham, Huntley Crouch, the late Petesey Edwards and Wilmot Irvin for their time, advice and encouragement.

Thank you, Mom and Dad, for reading to me, and for spoiling me with all the books I ever wanted. Thank you, Erin Wackerhagen, for capturing the image of the muffler man for my cover. Thanks also to Betty Roman and Pat Flanagan for transcribing previous drafts of this novel.

And finally, much thanks to my beloved hometown(s) of Fountainville and Simpson Inn, and their amazing inhabitants.